continued...

D0064542

"From assassination attempts to steamy sex scenes to the summoning of magical powers, Havens covers a lot of ground. Weaving together political intrigue, romance, and fantasy is definitely tricky, but Havens makes it work in this quick-paced, engaging story with unique and likable characters." —*Booklist*

"Mix the mystique of all three Charlie's Angels, Buffy's brass and scrappy wit, add the globe-trotting smarts of Sydney Bristow, and you might come up with enough cool to fill Bronwyn's little witchy finger... How can you not fall in love with a character who flies her own plane, combusts the bad guys with a flick of the wrists, and has a weakness for sexy men and deep-fried chicken?" —Britta Coleman, author of *Potter Springs*

"Smart, sexy, and sinfully wicked." —*USA Today* bestselling author Ronda Thompson

"This is a refreshing, fast-paced entry for Havens, who pulls out all stops to put the world to rights with humor, some good old-fashioned street fighting—witch style—and some well-deserved romance." —*Romantic Times*

"Bronwyn, the tough, sassy heroine in Candace Havens's *Charmed & Dangerous*, is one very wicked witch—as in wickedly clever, funny, sexy, and irresistible!" —Jennifer Archer, author of *Body & Soul*

"*Bewitched* meets Buffy meets Bond... Ms. Havens does a fantastic job with her debut into the world of romance." —*Romance Divas*

"Laugh-out-loud, sexy fun! Candace Havens is a sparkling new voice that will draw you in and hold you captive." —Gena Showalter, author of *Awaken Me Darkly*

"A bewitching read, full of easy humor and vivid descriptions. Debut novelist Candace Havens's refreshing style and clever story weaving will leave you eager for more charming and dangerous adventures." —Laurie Moore, Edgar® Award–nominated author of *Constable's Apprehension*

The
Demon King
and I

CANDACE HAVENS

BERKLEY BOOKS, NEW YORK

THE BERKLEY PUBLISHING GROUP
Published by the Penguin Group
Penguin Group (USA) Inc.
375 Hudson Street, New York, New York 10014, USA
Penguin Group (Canada), 90 Eglinton Avenue East, Suite 700, Toronto, Ontario M4P 2Y3, Canada
(a division of Pearson Penguin Canada Inc.)
Penguin Books Ltd., 80 Strand, London WC2R 0RL, England
Penguin Group Ireland, 25 St. Stephen's Green, Dublin 2, Ireland (a division of Penguin Books Ltd.)
Penguin Group (Australia), 250 Camberwell Road, Camberwell, Victoria 3124, Australia
(a division of Pearson Australia Group Pty. Ltd.)
Penguin Books India Pvt. Ltd., 11 Community Centre, Panchsheel Park, New Delhi—110 017, India
Penguin Group (NZ), 67 Apollo Drive, Rosedale, North Shore 0632, New Zealand
(a division of Pearson New Zealand Ltd.)
Penguin Books (South Africa) (Pty.) Ltd., 24 Sturdee Avenue, Rosebank, Johannesburg 2196,
South Africa

Penguin Books Ltd., Registered Offices: 80 Strand, London WC2R 0RL, England

This book is an original publication of The Berkley Publishing Group.

This is a work of fiction. Names, characters, places, and incidents either are the product of the author's imagination or are used fictitiously, and any resemblance to actual persons, living or dead, business establishments, events, or locales is entirely coincidental. The publisher does not have any control over and does not assume responsibility for author or third-party websites or their content.

PRINTING HISTORY
Berkley trade paperback edition / November 2008

Library of Congress Cataloging-in-Publication Data

Havens, Candace, 1963–
    The demon king and I / Candace Havens. — Berkley trade paperback ed.
        p. cm.
    ISBN 978-0-425-22363-5
    I. Title.

PS3608.A878D4 2008
813'.6—dc22

2008025609

PRINTED IN THE UNITED STATES OF AMERICA

10 9 8 7 6 5 4 3 2 1

To my sisters in crime

ACKNOWLEDGMENTS

Anne Sowards, your incredible insight made this book what it is. I could not have done it without you. Cameron Dufty, thank you for always being so patient and keeping up with the details. Leslie Gelbman and Susan Allison, I can't tell you how much I appreciate your belief in me.

Shannon Canard and Rosemary Clement Moore, I simply could not ask for better friends. You keep me sane. Curtis, your undying support and web mastery skills leave me in awe. Sha-Shana, please know you will always be golden to me.

To my readers: You rock beyond belief. Your letters and e-mails keep me going when times get tough. I hope you love the Caruthers sisters as much as I do.

PROLOGUE

The Guardian Keys have protected Earth since the beginning of time. It is our job to guard the portals and keep beings from other worlds away. We are peacekeepers and must often travel between dimensions to make sure everyone plays nice.

Each of us is given powers to help with our duties, and we are trained from birth to fight evil in all its forms. And damn if there aren't a lot of forms involved—between dragons, demons, nasty fairies, and sea nymphs, we have our hands full. The small tattoos we're born with on our wrists designate which worlds we are to negotiate with and guard against. Mine are stars, which means I'm in charge of the tough-skinned, hardheaded demons. Beings that would sooner kill you than look at you.

I know, you're really jealous right now.

Hey, it's my job. Most days it's not that bad. I jump through time and space, slice off a demon head or two, and boom, baby; I'm back in time for cocktails.

Then there are days when I come home beat up and covered in demon goo. Can't say those are my favorites.

Of course, just because we have to save the world doesn't mean we can't do it in a great pair of boots and the latest Marc Jacobs blouse. I mean, we girls should have some pleasures in life.

—Gillian Caruthers

CHAPTER

1

"I could kill him, but then I'd have to dispose of the body." I stared at myself in the mirror of my office bathroom willing the tears away. I was a complete wreck. "Murder *is* messy."

An hour earlier I'd walked in on Emilio, my lover, and Maria, the manager of one of the art galleries I own, going at it like monkeys in my São Paulo apartment.

I'd have to sell the place. Yuck, and that beautiful bed would have to be burned. I slammed the side of the sink and a piece of granite hit the ground. Oops.

Stupid superhuman strength.

Come on, Gillian. Get it together.

I met Emilio at a party at another gallery in Milan a few months ago and fell in love with his art, a mix of contemporary greats Anselm Kiefer and Julian Schnabel. I convinced him to come to Brazil for a showing in my new gallery.

While he finished the installation of the pieces, I had traveled to Texas for some business meetings. When I'm not dabbling in the arts and artists, I run my family's company, Caruthers Corporation. It keeps me busy, but with technology I'm always just a phone call or e-mail away.

My mother had the jet out, so I'd taken an early flight to Brazil so that I could surprise Emilio before the big show.

The artist was tall, dark, and brooding—exactly my type. I have a thing for complex men. His hair was shoulder length and so black it almost looked blue. He had an artist's body, long and lithe with sinewy muscles. And the sex was beyond amazing. Evidently, Maria thought so, too.

Ugh. Bile rose in my throat. It wasn't like me to get this torn up over a guy. *I must be tired.*

Sighing, I tried to push the memory of them wrapped around one another from my mind. I straightened my shoulders. Pulling a compact from my purse, I repaired the damage.

It wasn't easy, but I made myself smile. "No man is worth crying over." It was something Mom had lectured me and my three sisters about since we first noticed boys. "They are a tool for sexual satisfaction, and they are good companions. Nothing more." Mom never minced words, even when we were twelve. I'd probably be really warped if I hadn't seen how much she loved my father. They never agreed on anything, but there was a deep connection between them.

Mom had a different way of looking at the world than most people, but she had her reasons. She'd be really angry if she saw my tear-stained face as I stood hiding in the gallery bathroom.

I dabbed the powder under my eyes and then around my red nose. Taking another calming breath, I searched for my favorite MAC Solar Plum lipstick. The color made me smile, and I needed that right now.

After taking one last look, I straightened my little black halter dress and smoothed the tiny tendrils escaping from the chignon trapping the rest of my light brown curls.

The piece of granite went into the wastebasket. Opening the door, I slipped into the crowded gallery. My sister Alex had helped me transform the abandoned warehouse into a maze of large partial walls with the perfect lighting to show off the art. It was our second showing and all of São Paulo had arrived for the party.

With my best fake smile on my face I said hello to the guests.

"Gillian, you've done it again," said Mark Michikin, the editor of *Art* magazine. He was a harsh critic, so any praise was a small miracle.

Giving him a light squeeze on his arm, I air-kissed his cheek. "Wonderful. Are you having a good time? Looks like you need a new glass of champagne." I pointed to his empty glass and motioned to a waiter to replace it.

As I moved through the throng I spotted Emilio. He smiled and reached out to me. *Jerk.* It was obvious he and Maria hadn't noticed me watching them for the few seconds I caught their erotic act. They had arrived separately and were acting as if nothing had happened between them.

My smile faltered when I looked at him. I wasn't sure I could do this. We hadn't made our relationship exclusive, so he had the right to date whomever he wanted, but not the woman who managed my gallery. A woman I had trusted.

I could rip off her head. Pausing, I grabbed a glass of champagne and made myself take a sip. *Jeez, Gilly, that's a little drastic. Calm down.* I always had conversations in my head—it was the way I sorted out things—but usually they weren't so murderous in intent.

I willed myself to get Zen. Emilio had a strange look on his face, which meant he couldn't read mine.

Then it hit me. What was life without a Caruthers girl scandal? It'd had been awhile since the tabs had zeroed in on one of the four sisters. We were known for our parties, our men, and our jet-setting lives. It was a ruse we all perpetuated for the greater good. I was about to give the press, and the elite of São Paulo, the show of a lifetime. It would be great for business. People loved a scandal.

"And here, ladies and gentlemen, is the most beautiful woman in the world." Emilio opened his arms to embrace me and seemed startled when I handed him my champagne glass.

"Funny, did you say the same thing to Maria when you screwed her on my bed an hour ago?"

There was a collective gasp, as if I'd thrown cold water on the crowd. I'm usually the sister who shies away from public drama, preferring to keep the press guessing, but I was in a weird mood. Out of sorts, I guess, and I just couldn't stop myself.

"Bad form, Maria." I turned to look at her. "Biting the hand that feeds you. You really should have been here early to make sure everything was set up properly. I'm afraid your work ethic is going to be called into question." They both stepped back out of the circle, and the gallery went very quiet.

"Gillian, you are mistaken," Emilio sputtered.

Maria's jaw dropped. It wasn't very attractive. I decided right then that I'd really never liked her.

"No, I don't think so. I had a very good view of both of you. Maria, you may want to have that large mole on your back checked out." She blanched.

I paused and pointed at Emilio. "I suggest you get your things out of my house tonight, as I'm selling it in the morning."

"Gillian. You don't understand. I was using her as a . . ."

I gave him a wicked smile. "I know exactly what you were using her for, Em. I just don't like sharing my playthings. I'm selfish that way." The group around me snickered.

His frown made his brow crinkle, and I knew I'd struck something within him. He didn't like the idea of being a boy toy. Too bad.

Moving so that I stood toe-to-toe with Maria, I gave her another evil glare. "Security will be escorting you out. And I'm afraid there isn't going to be a severance package." I motioned to the guards by the door and they stood on each side of her.

"You can't—" she said in her heavy Portuguese accent.

"Oh, but I can. And if I were you, I'd go back to school and try a new career. I have a feeling you're going to have a very difficult time finding a job in any art gallery—anywhere in the world." No one in the room had any idea how much harm I could have caused her in that moment, and it wouldn't have fazed me.

She must have had some inkling I had murder on my mind, because her lips tightened to a thin line, and then she stared intently at her shoes.

I turned my back on her and kept my power in check.

"Gaston will see to your needs for the rest of the evening," I said to the crowd. "Please enjoy yourselves. Emilio is a cad and a cheat, but he's also very talented." I glanced at him patronizingly, as if he were a petulant child.

Gaston walked up to me. "Are you okay, Ms. Caruthers?" His face held genuine concern and it was almost my undoing.

I reached out and touched his arm. "I'm fine. Congratulations on your promotion, Gaston. Even if events hadn't gone the way they had, you deserved it. I've been very impressed with your performance the past few months." I smiled at him. "I'll call you later and check on the sales. Please make sure our guests have a wonderful evening."

"Yes, Ms. Caruthers."

"Oh, and something fell against the sink in my private washroom and broke it. Please have that replaced." No way could I tell him what had really happened.

He nodded.

After locking my office door, I stepped out the back through my private entrance. Touching the tiny star-shaped tattoos on my wrists together, I disappeared into the night.

A few seconds later I teleported into the control room at the family estate in Texas. This was the big hub where we lived and worked. The room felt cold after the heat of Brazil.

Straight ahead was a glassed-off portion where our security personnel monitored any dimension travelers. Jake, the head of our team, gave me a short wave before he turned back to the monitors.

Mira, my sister, waited for me. "What happened?" I heard the worry in her voice. One of Mira's many powers is that of psychic empathy. Anytime one of us experiences any strong emotional stress she picks up on it, no matter where she happens to be in the universe.

Dressed in khakis and a tank with big hiking boots, her bright red hair was tied in a knot at her shoulders. She'd probably been researching herbs in one of Earth's dying rain forests.

I pulled off my Christian Louboutin pumps and stepped onto the cold steel floor. It was grated and not very kind to narrow heels. "I'll tell you later." I motioned to the window, where three security men watched the screens in front of them.

They took incoming calls from Xerxes, Maunra, Kose, and Prent. The security team also kept an eye out for dimension jumpers on the state-of-the-art equipment my brilliant brother, Bailey, had designed.

My sisters and I were Guardian Keys protecting Earth from beings that shouldn't be here. Each of us had been blessed—or cursed, depending on how you looked at it—with magic and powers to help deal with a specific world. I was lucky enough to get the demon world Maunra. Yay, me.

We were born with the powers we needed, and in our late teens we were each assigned a world to correspond with our particular talent. Since I could rip demon heads off as easily as some people open a box of cereal, I had the pleasure of dealing with Maunra.

Circling my head, I tried to ease the tension from my neck. "I need to change. Why don't you make us some tea and I'll meet you in the kitchen? Do you have time? Were you in the middle of something?"

"I always have time for you, Gilly." Mira put a hand on my shoulder.

From the outside, the Caruthers enclave looked like a sixty-thousand-foot American Gothic–styled mansion, and it was. Only a chosen few knew there were several more levels beneath the three on top of the ground. That was where our security teams, weapons experts, and other people who helped us protect Earth worked. After going up two floors in the elevator, we stepped through the door into a carpeted hallway that led to the main house.

The great thing about being able to travel through space in the blink of an eye was that we four sisters could always be there for one another. It also helped us do our jobs more efficiently.

"Was it Emilio?" she finally asked.

I nodded.

"He's an idiot. Whatever he did. You know that, right?"

"Yes, he's definitely a moron. And he's no longer a factor in my life. I'm okay, I promise. I just need an hour or so to get myself back on track."

Mira stopped at the hallway leading off to the kitchen and dining areas. "I heard a rumor that Mom left some bread pudding in the fridge."

My head popped up. "I'll throw on something more comfortable and meet you there." I stopped. "Wait, Mom's cooking? Is she upset about something?"

Mira shrugged. "Don't know, but she's not here so don't worry." She smiled. "I love you, Gilly."

I hugged her. "I love you, too."

Once I was in my suite of rooms, I stripped everything off and put on a black silk robe. Pulling the pins from my hair, I shook out my shoulder-length curls and pushed them behind my ears.

My room was a soothing combination of blues and creams, with dark rich wood furniture. My sanctuary. I sat on the edge of my bed and assumed a meditation pose. I cleared my mind and searched for tabula rasa. It was difficult, as the anger at Em and Maria flared, but I let it go. They weren't worth the stress. Putting my hands in a prayer position, I concentrated on my breath. Eventually I found that lovely white space of nothingness. Ten minutes later, I was relaxed. I took a cleansing breath and released the last of the negativity.

My cell phone rang and I pulled it from my evening bag. Thinking it was Mira tempting me with dessert, I answered without looking.

"Hey."

"Ms. Caruthers, it's Jake with security. We have a message for you."

I fell back on the bed and my hand moved to my forehead. "Yes?"

"Ma'am, the demon king Arath requests your presence."

I rubbed my temples. "Now?" I sighed. *Stupid question, Gil, of course now. Demons didn't call for playdates.* "Arath? Wait—there's a new king?"

"Yes, ma'am."

Great. I shouldn't have been surprised. Maunra was overthrown every six months by whoever had garnered the most power. Bloody coups were business as usual there.

"I'll be down in a minute."

I grabbed the remote to open my closet door. Pushing the

fast-forward button, I watched as my wardrobe flew past on the electronic trolley.

New demon kings were known for being pompous and full of themselves. As a liaison between worlds, I had to be courteous and respectful of the new monarch. Of course, all bets were off if they happened to cross through a portal to Earth.

That's when I enjoyed my job the most. Nothing quite like going hand to claw with a Morgre demon who wanted you dead. Made me appreciate the simple things in life. Like slicing off the heads of the offending creatures.

This particular species of demon had so many breeds that you never knew what you might run into. The last demon king had been a Klon, a horned beast who could do little more than grunt but had the strength of Superman and then some.

It was important to dress ready for battle. On Maunra, women were considered equals, a good and a bad thing. They expected the women to fight to establish their status. If called to prove myself, I'd have to hold my own against the king—or his chosen one.

Picking clothes for kicking demon butt wasn't as easy. I needed something that would withstand the claws and teeth (they fought nasty), and I also had to be able to move fast.

I stopped the trolley at the leather section of my wardrobe. A leather bustier and pants with graphite inserts to keep the claws at bay.

My phone rang again. It was Mira.

"Don't eat all the bread pudding," I begged her. "I've got to meet a new demon king."

"No promises," she said with her mouth full. "This is good stuff. She used her special bourbon sauce. Sorry." She had the nerve to laugh. So much for sisterly love.

I growled. Now I was really mad.

Stupid demon king was making me miss my favorite dessert.

I'd killed for less.

CHAPTER

2

"Explain again why I'm in charge of the demon hordes?" I snapped a small vial of poison into my pants leg. One never knows when one might have to slip a death mickey into a demon's teacup, or mug of blood. The beverage depended on the creature du jour.

The weapons room at Caruthers Corp., a steel box with computers, metal tables, and no windows, was cold and I flexed my fingers to keep them warm.

Mira met me there with a small cup of bread pudding, all that was left after leaving her alone with a dish full of the stuff. "Well, you look really good in leather, and you have that lawyer's kind of patience, so very diplomatic when you need to be. And when all of that fails, you rock at kicking ass. I mean, no one rips off a demon head like you do, Hercugirl." She handed me my sword and pushed her long red hair behind her ear.

I winced at the Hercugirl comment. My sisters had tagged me with that name when my powers came in and we discovered I could pick up a small car with one hand. I could also run fast. My powers weren't that glamorous, but both helped against the demons.

Each of us also chose a profession to keep our real jobs a secret. When I told everyone I wanted to study law, they made fun of me, but it came in handy. I helped my mother run the family businesses, and I bailed out my siblings when they found themselves in trouble. I like the law; the logic of it just makes sense to me.

On the side I dabbled in art and the occasional artist. For some reason that kept the creative side of me happy.

I sheathed my sword in the back harness. "I do like that ripping-heads-off part a lot." Winking at her, I reached for the new infrared guns we'd been testing and put them in the holsters at my hips. Bailey, our brilliant and ornery brother, had made them. They were heavier than I would have liked, but they could blow up a demon faster than any bullet.

"Did they say exactly why they wanted you to come tonight?" She turned to the computer and typed in several codes. A panel on the wall opened and a tiny box popped out. Her slim fingers lifted what looked like a black watch with a large dial and she moved to put it around my wrist.

"It has something to do with the new king taking power,

more a formality, and me showing respect, than anything. While I'm there, maybe I can convince him to shut down all the portals to keep his demon scum on the right side."

Mira shrugged. "If anyone can do it, you can."

I pulled on a leather jacket from the metal hook behind me. With the sword at my back it was a snug fit, but it worked.

We use the tattoos—each of us has a different design—imprinted on our wrists to go back and forth on Earth. The "watch" helped focus and magnify our natural power when going to other worlds. It opened portals that made traveling much easier. If we tried to do it on our own, there was a good chance of winding up dead floating around the universe.

That was never a good thing.

The devices we call watches (even though they don't tell time) were devised by my brother and had made travel to other dimensions safer. The technology had been borrowed from another world hundreds of years ago, but my brother had a way of improving on things. Before he tweaked the system, we'd land on the other side wiped out, which was difficult when we arrived in the middle of a hostile situation. Now we landed fresh as flowers. Or at least as fresh as a flower who'd had a three-martini lunch would be.

Pushing the tiny button on the side of the watch, I lifted it toward the wall in front of me. A hazy fog developed and then a rush of cold wind brushed past. Think *Stargate*, but on a much smaller scale. A fine blue circle emerged and I moved forward.

Darn. I slapped myself mentally. "Listen, I know it's not your job, but could you make sure Mom signs the papers I left on her desk? There's a meeting with Harrison in the morning and I don't know if I'll have a chance to talk with her before then. I could be a while if there's a big reception for the new king on Maunra. Oh, and I left some briefs in the blue folder she should probably take a look at." A lawyer's work was never done. "Georgia was supposed to have the final guest list ready for the Arts in Schools Ball. Make sure Alex gets a copy." Georgia was my executive assistant and I couldn't live without her.

Mira made a swishing motion with her hands. "I'll take care of it. Go and play with your stinky demons."

I snorted. "Fine." Stepping through the circle was always a strange feeling. My stomach did this weird thing for half a second as my DNA traveled faster than the speed of light and then dumped me, usually rump first, on the ground.

This time I landed feet first, and it was a good thing. Three Tresk demons stood before me. I'm tall, but the horned, hooded-eyed beasts had at least a foot on me.

"*Nok to stord mid tonga.*" The greenish one on the left motioned toward a path.

Argh. I'd forgotten to hook in the earpiece that translates their language, another Bailey invention. Unzipping the front left pocket of my jacket, I put the translator in my ear.

He repeated the phrase. "You follow us to castle." *Ah, much better.*

Most people believe demons live in a hellish world and are evil. True, they are ill-tempered and would sooner kill you than look at you, but they have a code they live by and are honorable beings in their own weird way. And their world is actually freezing cold, hence the need for toasty leather and a great pair of boots.

The green demon, who really needed an Altoid, led the way and the other two followed behind me.

I'd landed at the edge of the royal roost, which meant we had to walk about two hundred yards through twisted trees to get to the castle.

As we broke through to the end of the path, the world opened up, and against the grayish purple sky sat a huge medieval castle. I'd been here many times to speak with the hardheaded Shctock, the former king. He treated me like an invader and tried to find a way to kill me every time I stopped by. Not once in the six months I'd dealt with him did he ever do anything I asked. Can't say I was sad he'd died, but I wasn't really looking forward to meeting Arath.

Mira had done some quick research on the new guy, but all we found out was he was a lethal warrior who had put together the armies to defeat Shctock. The fact that he had requested my presence could be a good sign or not. I was pre-pared either way.

"You go." The green demon pushed me toward the humon-gous wooden doors. "His Majesty wants talk."

I smiled at him. "Thank you." *Don't kill the demon. Don't*

kill the demon. I don't like being pushed or touched in any way, especially by demons. It made me cranky.

I'm not sure why, but I'd expected a big reception for the new king. When I walked through the doors, no one was there. I'd imagined at the very least that the elders from all of the demon clans would be groveling at his hooves or something.

The heels of my boots echoed in the empty hall. Iron sconces lit the walls and a fire had been built in a fireplace that was as tall as me. Needing the warmth, I headed toward it.

"You are smaller than I imagined." The voice was rich and deep and it spoke perfect English. I knew this because I heard him in my left ear as well as the right, which had the translator.

I turned but didn't see anything. *You are much more invisible than I imagined.* I thought the words, but didn't say them aloud. No need to be rude right away. Instead I cleared my throat. "Hello?"

I saw a quick movement to my left and then he appeared, standing next to one of the large tapestries hanging from the ceiling. I'm five ten, but he was at least six feet five with extremely broad shoulders.

Totally racist of me, but I'd expected scales. Most of the demons I'd encountered in my world and on Maunra were big ugly monsters. There. I said it. Think the worst of me.

But this was not an ugly monster. He was gorgeous from his short auburn hair and smooth bronze skin to his ripply muscles under his vest-covered chest. He looked more like a pirate on one of my sister Alex's favorite romance novels.

"They tell me you can break a Norg in two." He walked toward me in his jeans, Levi button-fly, to be exact, not that I glanced at his crotch or anything. *Who is this guy?*

I slipped on my lawyer mask to cover the surprise-filled one I'm sure had hit my face for a split second, and smiled. "Hi, I'm Gillian Caruthers." I waved rather than shook hands.

In the demon world if you offer your hand, it can mean all sorts of things, from agreeing to birth demon babies to being someone's dinner. It's just not safe to shake hands. I'd learned that long ago.

He made a slight bow. "I am honored to meet the Guardian Key." He raised a large hand and waved back to me. "I am Arath."

Whew. The new demon king was a hot bod. There had to be something weird under the jeans.

I bet he has a tail or two—

Ack, Gillian.

"Your eyes show surprise. Perhaps you think me unbearable to look at, as I sport no scales."

It was almost as if he had read my mind. *Yikes.* I know it's not physically possible, but my tongue twisted into a knot. All I could do was shake my head no.

Finally I found my voice. "Your appearance is quite appealing, King Arath, and I offer my respect and congratulations for your new position."

His eyes flashed orange and then back to brown. It was the only indication I'd seen so far of his demonic heritage. "You find me appealing?"

"Uh, um." *Okay, lawyer brain, kick in any time here.* "I don't find you displeasing." *Change the subject.* "I understand you wanted to see me. I thought perhaps there would be a reception honoring you tonight."

He moved closer now, and I smelled something strange, a musky scent, not unpleasant, with a touch of cloves. It made my stomach do strange fiddly things and I wanted to touch him, an unusual reaction to a demon for me, as I usually had an urge to kill them.

He didn't speak.

I straightened my shoulders. "There are many things I'd like to discuss with you."

He walked around me in a circle. Then he paused. "Follow me." Striding to the other end of the hall, he motioned me toward another wooden door. "The fire is warm here and we can talk."

A demon king who wants to talk? It was beyond crazy, in a good way.

A million things ran through my mind. I needed to speak with him about the portals. That was paramount, but I had so many questions. How had he learned English? The queen's English, to be precise. He sounded as if he'd been educated at Oxford. What clan did he belong to—and did they all look like him? How had he defeated the king and where was everyone?

I'd never been in this castle when there weren't at least fifty demons roaming the great hall. It had always been a loud and boisterous place full of danger, until now.

He turned and gave me a strange look, one I couldn't decipher. *It's still a dangerous place, Gilly.*

The room we entered had a wooden table surrounded by thronelike chairs with intricate carvings of scary fanged beasts. "Sit." He pointed to the chair nearest the fire. This room had stone walls with only the sconces and the fire for light.

There was a weariness in his eyes, the kind of tired that spoke of many battles and a warrior who'd been fighting for too long.

"I do not celebrate death. That is why there is no reception. Shctock would not listen to reason. That is why he is dead. I did not wish to be king, but change was necessary, and I trust no other."

Well, okay then.

"I understand." I scooted back in the chair, feeling like a child whose feet couldn't touch the ground. "Change is never easy and this must have been a difficult time for all involved."

He snorted. "You understand nothing, Guardian, but it matters not. You want the portals closed, and I'm agreeable to this."

I was immensely pleased. In a matter of seconds I'd accomplished more than I had in the last few years with the other demon kings. And it had been his idea. I didn't want to play devil's advocate, but it was necessary to find out why this demon king wanted the portals closed. "You agree? What about the freedom of your people to jump dimensions?"

"They are not welcome in your world, and die if they dare to enter. Is this not true?"

"I only kill when necessary." Which was almost always, but I didn't want to tell him that.

"I protect my people by keeping them from your world, where you would butcher them."

The conversation had taken an odd turn, one I wasn't terribly comfortable with, but I kept my temper.

"I only kill them when they harm the humans or do things they shouldn't. This began before my time or yours. The demons cause great havoc in my world and that is unacceptable."

"Is this why you killed my mother?" His face was a mask of control and I wondered if I'd imagined the words.

I coughed. "Excuse me? I think I would know if I had killed your mother." It would have come up when we did research on him before this trip.

"Your father did." He shoved away from the table, knocking the chair back, and paced in front of the fireplace. "He would not grant her reentry into our world, and she grieved for us. So much so that her heart broke and she died. That is the story our father tells us. That is the reason my brother, Throe, and I became warriors, to make our mother proud. I despise the humans."

It seemed an odd comment since up close he looked very human to me.

He shoved an angry hand through his hair. A strange yellow aura surrounded him. *Okay, maybe not so human.*

"You must go. I will call for you another day." The words were soft but menacing. His back was still to me.

I'd been dismissed.

"Look, I'm sorry about what happened. My father is dead, but he believed in family and how important it is that we all stick together. It would go against everything he stood for to keep a mother from her children. I will find out what happened and bring you the truth the next time you call." I spoke the words with confidence I didn't feel.

"You dare say my father speaks falsehoods? I do not need your version of the truth. Go!" The words roared from his mouth like from a great lion gone mad. Energy burst around the castle and before I could move, five guards appeared, all holding their swords at the ready.

Demons can move really fast when they want to.

Knowing my life would be in danger if I stayed a moment longer, I moved past them as fast as I could. At the front doors, I broke into a run and pushed the button on my watch to open the portal.

Great. The demon king hates my guts. Oh, well, nothing new there.

I jumped through the portal and landed in the weapons room with a big thud.

Mira had gone and I was glad. I needed a moment just to collect my thoughts and to breathe.

God, that was intense. Nothing like running from a horde of demons to get the adrenaline pumping. I shrugged out of the leather jacket and put the weapons I'd been carrying away. Back in my room I changed from the leather outfit into some jeans and a yellow Theory blouse.

Arath was wrong about his mother. My father would never have kept someone from returning home through one of the portals. We were always happy to get the demons out of our world. Arath's father had lied to him and I wanted to know why.

One thing my dad did well was keep excellent records of everything to do with this world and the others we guard against. Before I spoke with my mom, I wanted to check to see if he had logged anything about the incident.

Touching my tattoos together, I arrived in my office on the thirtieth floor of the building in downtown Austin where the Caruthers Corp. has its headquarters. It's the place where I spend the majority of my time when I'm home.

Being the daughter of the boss had its privileges. The corner office was large and looked out over the city. The walls were burnished gold and the tables, desk, and chairs were stained mahogany. All of the furniture was upholstered with a beautiful bronze fabric my sister Alex had found in Paris. She, who was known for designing the world's best party palaces, had put this space together for me and I loved it.

I turned the plasma TV on to CNN for some company, and flipped through the folders on the desk, looking for the papers my mom was supposed to sign and get back to me. They weren't there. She'd probably left them in her office; I decided to check later.

I sat down at the computer and typed in my password. The initial search on the new demon king hadn't given me much information, but I hadn't been looking for his heritage. I was more than curious now. I'd never met anyone like him, especially from the demon world.

I found the brief summary Mira had printed out earlier. I clicked through to the next page and read about Arath's father. Kildenren had been a fierce warrior and the chief of his clan. He'd died fighting in the Keepers War. Religion, something strange to associate with demons, was at the basis of many of their wars, much like here at home. The Keepers had tried to take over, but the other demon clans had banded together to keep their freedom.

Tapping my fingers on the mouse, I clicked to the next page. Kildenren's mate, Juliet Morrison, was listed with two children, Arath and Throe.

I couldn't believe what I read. It couldn't be the same person. I put the cursor on her name. It was. I knew her as Aunt Juliet, who was human, and the last time I checked, she was very much alive.

CHAPTER

3

My hands shook a little with the news and I sat back in my leather chair. How could she have left her children behind?

Aunt Juliet's only faults, up until now, were that she was too kind and had terrible taste in men. That happened to be something we had in common. She wasn't my real aunt, but she and my mother had been friends since long before I was born. When my dad died a few years ago, it was Juliet who helped put the family back together. A generous and loving person, she was not the sort of woman to abandon children.

The Morrisons were another family of Guardians, and for many years Juliet and her sisters had done the same thing the

Caruthers did. All of the sisters had eventually retired to marry and raise children. Well, except for Juliet. She was the life of every party and refused to spend too much time with any one man. She'd also become a powerful mage. Not as strong as my mother, but she definitely had a way with magic.

I picked up the phone and dialed Mom's office on the off chance she might still be there. No answer. I wanted to call Juliet, but what would I say—hey, why did you leave your demon babies behind?

I hated when I judged people before I had all the facts. If she had left her children behind, she'd had a reason. A good one. But I couldn't just come out and ask her about it. I needed to talk to Mom.

She didn't answer when I called, which was weird since she never turned off her phone. Maybe she was in the sauna or having dinner at the club. They wouldn't allow phones in there. Honestly, she could be anywhere in the universe. As a powerful mage, her services were always in need. She was also good at keeping up the Caruthers ruse. Most people in our circle of friends thought she was the successful, polished business-woman she appeared to be. She was that and so much more.

"Hey, sis, working hard or hardly working?" Bailey's voice surprised me and I almost fell back in my chair.

"Jesus, Bailey! You scared the hell out of me." I'd been so wrapped up in my thoughts I hadn't noticed his reflection in the window.

"Ooooh, I scared the big bad demon slayer." He licked his finger and painted an imaginary tick mark. "Chalk one up for Bailey Boy."

I cleared my throat, my eyebrow twitching. We don't talk about our other jobs in public. Ever.

"I know the rules, Gilly, but no one's around." He waved a long arm. "As usual you are the last one left. Have you seen Mom?"

"No. I don't know where she is. I just tried to call her phone. What are you doing here so late?"

Bailey sat down in one of the chairs facing my desk. My brother is a good-looking guy. Oh, not by my standards, but twice he's been voted the "Hottest Bachelor" in *In Scene* magazine. He has curly blond hair that always needs to be cut and he lives in jeans and retro T-shirts. Especially fond of any that sport shows from the Cartoon Network, he always looks like he's just rolled out of the wrong side of bed.

To me, he's the world's biggest dork. Smart, but a dork just the same.

"I've been working on the new underwater camera for Claire. She needs it next week for the tiger shark shoot. I've got to work on the lens and focus options, but it's close."

I almost asked Bailey about Juliet but my computer beeped and I glanced at the screen. "Oh, crap."

"What?" Bailey leaned forward.

"I forgot about the Windrige fund-raiser tonight. I've canceled on their last two parties. Argh! Technically, I'm supposed to be in São Paulo at the gallery, and flying home, so I'm not expected. Bothers me, though, that I totally forgot about it."

Bailey leaned his elbows on my desk. "Mira said you and Emmy baby are on the outs." Secrets didn't last long in my family no matter how hard you begged someone not to tell. My brother didn't think much of my former Latin lover. In fact, he seldom appreciated my taste in men. I used to think it was that brotherly thing, looking out for his big sister and all that, but I'm beginning to believe he just had really good instincts when it came to the jerks I dated.

"Don't look so smug, poodle head." I sneered. "I kind of liked him. Sort of. Well, since I'm already over him, evidently I didn't care as much as I thought," I confessed, and he watched with his genius eyes.

This was what we did. He listened, made fun, and we moved on.

"What time did it start?" Bailey stood and stretched.

"What?" I was lost in my diatribe and forgot what we'd been talking about.

"Gilly, for a smart girl...the fund-raiser?"

"Oh, nine. But I don't want to go. Besides, it might look suspicious if I show up, after being in Brazil four hours ago."

"It's not even ten yet; the party will be going strong." He waggled his eyebrows. "Today's your lucky day, big sis. I've been trying to get in the same room with Katy Harrison for weeks. I saw her on the beach at Cannes, and she wears bikini bottoms like nobody else."

It took me a minute to realize that he meant she'd been tanning topless.

"You're such a perv, but thanks. Someone from the family should be there. Be careful with Katy—I have a meeting with her dad in the morning and I want to be able to look him in the eyes." I pointed a finger at him. "Whatever you do, don't get thrown into jail."

My brother had a tendency to live in his own world, a place that had a different set of rules than the ones the rest of us followed. Part of it had to do with his extremely logical brain. Unfortunately, the police didn't like it when he told them that they were wrong.

Bailey glanced down at his clothes. "I can be ready in thirty minutes. I've got to throw my tux in the steamer. I accidentally crammed it in a desk drawer."

Bailey "accidentally" did stuff all the time. Once his mind began a project, he became totally focused. Ordinary, everyday things, like dry cleaning and showers, tended to be forgotten.

A half hour later we walked toward the parking garage.

"Let me guess, you want me to drive you to the hotel and take your car to the house?" I took the keys he held out.

"Got it in one, Gilly. That way I can drink up my courage to talk to Katy, and when I fail miserably I won't be able to drive my drunk self home."

I laughed. "Just remember her eyes are above her chest. Women like it when you look them in the face."

He laughed at that.

Bailey headed to his Mercedes SL600 Roadster. His was black. Mine was red. Dad had given them to us for Christmas three years ago. Bailey had rigged it so they both worked as hybrids.

I preferred my truck, but the Mercedes was easier to park, and I didn't like listening to the lectures from Mira and Claire about how I was hurting the planet by using my fossil-fuel-chugging machine. So I only used the truck when I had to haul something.

The event was at the Driscoll, only a few blocks away. The valet opened the door, but I didn't move. "Not staying, Ms. Caruthers?" He reached a hand to help me out.

"Not tonight, Darryl. You never saw me, okay?"

It took him a second, but he nodded his head and smiled. "Okay."

"Make sure my brother gets a ride home or stays in our suite. He plans on drinking tonight."

He laughed. "I'll alert the staff to catch him before anything unfortunate happens."

The last time Bailey was drunk at the Driscoll he tried to slide down the banister. It hadn't been so difficult when he was a kid, but as a nonsober adult it didn't go as well. He'd had thirteen delicate and well-placed stitches after that escapade. "His future children will thank you."

I pulled out onto Sixth Street and considered grabbing some take-out Mexican, but I didn't feel like stopping. It had been a really long day and I was ready to get home.

I called ahead to the house and Mrs. Pompson, the house chef, picked up the phone. "Yes, Ms. Gillian."

"Hi, Mrs. Pompson, is there anything for dinner? What did you guys have tonight?" She oversaw a large staff that made certain everyone at the house was fed well. Since the complex was out in the middle of nowhere it didn't make sense for employees to have to drive twenty minutes for meals. There was also a well-stocked break room with snacks and drinks on the lowest level.

"Tonight we have a choice of chicken enchiladas and tortilla soup, or meat loaf and mashed potatoes."

They both sounded good.

"Excellent. I'll be home in fifteen minutes. I've been craving your enchiladas."

"We'll see you soon, miss. I added some habanero peppers to the sauce for you, just in case you made it home this evening."

I smiled. I loved that woman. She'd been working for the family for as long as I could remember, and she always seemed to know what we wanted. She shared the kitchen with my mother, which was no easy task. My mother loved to cook, and she worked out her stress by creating new recipes. It was absolutely the only domestic thing about her.

Mom was the one who taught us to fight and use weapons, while other children learned hopscotch and jumped rope. She was a tough broad, but we loved her.

My dad was the softhearted nurturer. The one who made certain we developed the social skills needed to travel in the circles we did. Fae, demons, dragons, Nereids, and other other-worldly beings were drawn to the rich and powerful, and that's where we often found the craftiest of them. Some had been in our world for centuries without detection; others tried to jump in more recently. It was our job to get rid of them, in whatever way possible.

Their crimes were often written off as serial killings or unexplained phenomena. People on Earth didn't want to believe in monsters, and I couldn't blame them.

I was so caught up in my thoughts that I didn't see the tail at first. It was only as I pulled onto the freeway that I noticed the black SUV speeding up on my bumper.

"Crap. Damn paparazzi."

I couldn't let them snap a photo, as I should have been headed home on a plane from Argentina. Since I was in my brother's car there was a good chance they thought I was his latest chick du jour.

Stamping my foot down on the accelerator, I shifted gears. They were gaining on me, and it would be tough to lose them on the highway. I shifted and made a quick exit and U-turn under the freeway, leading them back toward the university.

Winding my way through the back roads, I drove like a crazy woman on a mission. Ten minutes later I was free of the tail and jumped back on the highway.

My phone rang again.

"Ms. Caruthers, it's Jake. We have jumpers. The first one is a mile ahead of your current location on the right side. It's as if he is waiting for you."

Crap. "Got it. I'll intercept. Thanks." I checked the rearview to make sure the tail was really gone. Photographing me killing a demon would make the front page. I couldn't let that happen.

I turned onto the farm road leading to the house, and I pulled off on the shoulder. Popping the trunk, I went in search of weapons. Bailey had a Magnum in the trunk along with a bowie knife and some weird-looking machine. I had no idea what it did and had no time to figure it out.

I stuffed the knife in the back of my jeans and put the gun on the seat beside me.

As I turned the ignition, I was already planning how I could pin the demon between the eyes and split his brain open.

First it was the bread pudding. Now I had to postpone dinner. I have anger issues when I don't eat on a regular basis. Dad used to say it had something to do with my metabolism and blood sugar. The longer I went without eating, the more ferocious and mean I became.

Poor guy had no idea who he'd messed with tonight.

CHAPTER

4

"What the hell are you doing here?" I stomped out of the car. He was lucky I hadn't run him over.

Arath stood dressed much the same way as before, only now he had on a black long-sleeved T-shirt instead of the leather vest.

Those abs can't be real.

He looked like a hot biker guy. My traitorous body warmed at the sight of him, which only pissed me off more. He wasn't more than a mile from the Caruthers estate on our private road.

"I am demon king. I can pass through without warning."

"Yes, but we consider it a courtesy to message us before you jump, so we don't accidentally kill you."

He made a low growling sound. "It was not my choice. I did not have time for niceties. The magic is weakened around the portal and the more powerful of my kind are finding ways through."

"Jesus." That was the last thing I needed tonight. Idiot demons on killing sprees.

"I do not know this Jesus." His voice stern, he glared at me. For some reason, it just made me laugh. I chuckled so hard I bent over.

"This Jesus is funny?" He stood beside me.

I didn't think it possible but I laughed harder.

Arath watched me with a strange look on his face. "I do not understand your mirth."

"Sorry. It's been a long day, and I don't have time to explain." I flipped open my phone. "Jake, I've located jumper one, it's Arath. Where are the others?"

"I have one in Burbank near City Walk and another in Portugal. We're tracking both."

"I need you to send someone to pick up Bailey's car."

"Yes, ma'am."

I'd tried to get Jake to stop saying 'ma'am' two years ago when he started working for us, but he was a hard-core southern gent from Georgia, and he wasn't about to stop.

I faced Arath. "Do you have weapons?"

"I do not need weapons to kill."

I looked at his hands. He was probably right.

I was bummed that all I had was the gun and the knife. I

really loved my sword, but there just wasn't time. I was also without any body armor. Oh, well, at least I had Arath on my side.

I ran around to the trunk to grab one more thing. I'd seen some security badges in the back of Bailey's car. One never knew when something like that might come in handy.

I returned to Arath.

"Touch my shoulder."

He did and the heat from his hand burned through my body. I touched my star tattoos together and we whirled through space.

We landed hard in the parking lot of Universal Studios. Arath bumped into a Land Rover and the alarm went off. Startled, he started to put a fist through the hood.

I yanked on his arm. "It's just an alarm. Come on." I took off running, and he followed. Guardians had built-in trackers. Hard to explain but it was like a GPS in my brain. I sensed the direction in my mind and my feet followed.

Arath sniffed the air and pointed toward the *Mummy* attraction. I hoped the screams I heard were from the ride and not demon induced.

"Hey!"

We both turned to see a teenage girl pointing at Arath. "Do you work on the pirate ride? Man, I don't remember seeing you there."

Arath glanced down at me as if she were speaking gibberish.

I could see how she would mistake him for a pirate, even though he was in a T-shirt and jeans. He had that look, with the hair and the muscles. "He does, but he's off tonight. You'll have to look for him tomorrow." I wrapped my arm around his. "Come on, honey, we'll be late for dinner."

Arath stared at me with a strange look, but nodded.

The disappointed teen turned to her friends. "That bites. We'll have to pay to come back and see him tomorrow."

The girl screwed up her face as if she were upset, but they soon left.

"You go around the back. I'll start here," I whispered as we moved away from the small group of twittering teens.

He nodded and took off at a pace that surprised me. For a big man, he moved at cheetah speed.

I jumped over the gate and pushed through the throng of sweaty park visitors. There were some dirty looks, and a few mumbled, "Where does she think she's going?" I finally made it up to where the passengers lined up to get on the ride.

Careful to put my thumb over the photo, I pulled out a Homeland Security badge I'd found in Bailey's trunk. I flipped it at the ride attendant who directed passengers to the correct lines. "We have a situation, but I don't want to create a panic. I need you to bring the remaining passengers in, and close down the ride. Put up your maintenance sign. Stay calm and do not panic; we don't want people freaking out." I doubted an officer of the law would say "freaking out," but I hoped he didn't notice.

He stared at me dumbfounded. I had a feeling he wasn't accosted by Homeland Security every day.

I gave the kid a stern look. "Do you understand?"

He nodded. His freckled face was red with panic. "Do you think it's a dirty bomb?"

The kid watched too much Discovery Channel.

"We won't know until we get in there. Just keep the area clear." I stuffed the badge into my back pocket, and made a note to ask Bailey how he'd come across that one. Knowing him, he'd probably won it in a poker game.

He pointed to me. "Anyone ever tell you that you look like—"

Ride Boy also read too much *People*. He'd recognized me. "I get that all the time. As if." I rolled my eyes. "She's way prettier."

He nodded as if he agreed, and I turned before he could see my smile. Using my magic senses I climbed under the track and raced toward the demon. A strange noise caught my attention. *"Nok kad ma nos,"* I heard it chanting. I didn't need my translator, because I didn't care what he said. He had to die.

I hoped that was the final train that had just whizzed over my head. The last thing I needed was parkgoers watching the freak show that was about to happen. After it passed, I pulled myself up onto the track, then walked gingerly along the outside rails.

The Norst demon sat in the middle of the Pharaoh's treasure. If I hadn't been so pissed about missing my dinner, I might have laughed.

"It's fake," I yelled.

He ignored me and continued filling the small bags at his sides with fake rubies, diamonds, and sapphires. *Idiot.*

I tossed a plastic goblet at his head. "I'm talking to you."

He turned and growled. "*Blin.*"

"Blin? I'll show you blin, running around in a public place like this." I pulled the Magnum from the back of my belt and aimed it at his head.

He jumped so fast I didn't see him coming. His large scaly arm knocked me back against another chest of treasure. The gun flew out of my hand and tumbled beneath the tracks.

Jeez, that hurt. I'd have to do this the old-fashioned way. Hand-to-claw combat. He'd turned his back as if he didn't have to worry about me trying to kill him. Anger forced my muscles into action. I kicked the back of his right and then left knee. The big oaf fell forward.

"I don't like being touched." I jumped on his back and brought the bowie knife to his neck. He tried to reach around to pull me off. When that didn't work he began slamming his fist into my left arm. My right arm was free to shove the knife up through his jaw and soft palate and into his brain. I used my strength to twist it inside his skull and he did a face plant into the treasure he'd tried to steal.

"That was a good kill." Arath stood over me. "It is a Norst from the Bagled clan."

"I know." I let go of the knife and pushed myself up. Kicking the demon over, I pulled the weapon out and his face collapsed. Beyond the horrid smell, there was always a lot of green goo that stuck to everything. I can't tell you how many clothes I have to throw away; there was no way I could explain the mess to the dry cleaner's.

"Can you take him back to Maunra for me? I'll go after the other one. This guy could have caused major damage if he hadn't been so enamored with his treasure."

"He was a fool. The jewels are not real." *Chalk one up for Arath.* "I will hunt with you, once I have disposed of the Norst."

"No. I'm better on my own. Just keep the rest from crossing over."

He looked ready to argue, but stopped. "You are injured."

I stared down at my arm, which had a large gash from the demon's claws. *Crap.* I hadn't felt it, but it bled profusely.

Arath reached out and put his hand over the wound. A golden light flowed around the spot and the skin began to regenerate and close. The bruises and the blood disappeared. *Wow.*

"You're a healer."

He frowned. "Yes, but my people do not know. One cannot be a healer and a leader. To lead, one must be a warrior."

I understood. Strength was more important than anything to demons. *Never show weakness.* It was also a part of our
Caruthers creed.

I shook my head. "Your secret is safe with me. Thank you."

He cocked his head and gave me a strange look, almost as
if he were amused. "I closed and locked all of the portals once
you left. Someone on this side is letting them through."

Trying to ease the tension building in my brain, I rubbed
my temples with the tips of my fingers. "Okay. Once I catch
the demon in Portugal, I'll see what's causing the problem
with the portals. The last thing I need right now is a damn
demon infestation."

Arath frowned. "I do not wish my people in your world any
more than you do."

God, when will I stop offending the guy? "Arath, my apologies.
I did not choose my words wisely, and there is no excuse for
that."

He grabbed the demon with one hand and slung it over his
shoulder. *"Gorstat."* He said the word and a portal opened. *Holy
cow, Wonder Woman.* I was powerful, but I'd never seen anyone
open a portal with just a word.

This guy was just full of surprises.

It wasn't hard to spot the other Norst demon in
the middle of Marialva, Portugal. He stood out in front of a
sixteenth-century parish church. I'd been there with Alex

when she studied Gothic architecture. Most people thought of Portugal as a place with beautiful beaches, and it was, but up in the rocky hillside towns there were some incredibly wonderful buildings. Some more than a thousand years old.

So when I saw the seven-foot-tall scaly beast trying to beat down one of the beautiful wooden doors to get into St. James Church, I couldn't let him.

After Burbank, I'd made a quick stop back at the control room to get my sword. In less than two minutes I'd traveled from the ride at Universal to Portugal. It's a tough job, but someone has to do it.

"Get away from there. You're going to break something!" I screamed at him. It was five o'clock in the morning so there wasn't anyone on the street except the beast and me.

He continued to bang on the door and didn't even bother acknowledging my presence. Stupid monster. I brought my sword up and to the left and made a fast arching swing as I leapt and sliced off his head.

Sometimes killing a demon was as easy as that.

An hour later I'd showered, changed, and eaten a plateful of chicken enchiladas. Exhausted, I finally tumbled into bed.

It was difficult to believe that I had begun my day anxious to have a reunion with Emilio. That hadn't gone quite the way I expected. I didn't feel any more anger, which was weird.

It bothered me that I couldn't even muster up a tear for my short affair with Emilio. *Am I ever going to care about a man enough to mourn when he's gone?* My anger earlier had been more about having to share a plaything, and feeling betrayed, than the ending of a relationship. *You're a cold-hearted bitch.* That had come from the mouth of the guy I'd had an affair with a few weeks before Emilio. Ted, the comic book artist. *What was I thinking?* He was so clingy that by the third date I mentioned he wasn't my type, and maybe he needed some hobbies so he didn't obsess about the women he dated. He didn't appreciate my advice.

My mind shifted to Arath. I'd never seen such a gorgeous, chiseled face. That strong chin, and that mouth were beyond anything I'd seen on Earth. He was about as close to perfection as a guy could get. The way the right side of his mouth quirked up when I thanked him for healing me still made butterflies flutter in my stomach.

Thankfully, when I returned to the control room I discovered Arath had in fact closed the portals from his side with some strong magic. There hadn't been a sign of any more intruders, which was why I decided to take a break.

Sighing, I punched my pillow. "Just because he's good-looking doesn't mean it's okay to lust after him, Gils. He's a demon. It's your job to make sure he keeps the damn portals closed, and that's it."

I remembered how gentle he'd been when he healed my

arm, and the look of genuine concern when he realized I'd been hurt.

There was definitely more to the demon king than met the eye. I just wished I wasn't so damned eager to find out what other secrets he held.

CHAPTER

5

The dreams always began with a pool of blood. My vision blurred for a moment and then I saw her. Well, the back of a head with long blonde hair. I assumed it was a woman from the lithe build and delicate hands with long broken fingernails. She'd put up a fight.

Something about her hair seemed familiar. My breath caught for a moment, and my body shook. *No. No.* At first I thought it might be Claire, but her blonde hair was much lighter.

Someone had killed this poor woman and all I could think about was how grateful I was that it hadn't been my sister.

Think.

From the size of the black-red stain on the carpet, the other side of her had to be a disaster.

It's a dream. Wake up. Stop looking at the body.

I turned my head and saw the moon casting shadows on the floor. Thankfully I couldn't smell the blood. I took a deep breath and tried to take in all the details. The room was bare except for a bed with a garish green, orange, and red diamond-motif cover, an old television, and beat-up wooden tables. *A motel.* A lamp lay shattered on the floor. A notepad printed with the words "A-1 Motel" lay on the pieces of glass.

She'd tried to stave off her attacker with the lamp, and it had been smashed against the wall.

I never understood how I knew these things, I just did. There was another room to the right and I could see a sink through the door. I couldn't move in these dreams, but I tried anyway. Nothing happened. It was if I were a fly on the wall.

"Tell me your name." Sometimes when I asked I could get a glimpse of letters or a whisper of sound.

"Soon, Guardian." A disembodied voice penetrated the darkness, and the force of it made me jump.

I woke in a tangle of sheets, my body covered in sweat. *Well, that was different.* I'd never heard the killer's voice before. Leaning across the pillows, I reached to the nightstand and grabbed my cell.

The clock on the phone read 4:00 a.m.

He would love me for this one.

*   *   *

I left a message on Private Detective Kyle Mendez's phone and was just about to dial our head of security, Jake, when mine rang.

"Kyle?"

"Do you know what time it is?" His voice was rough with sleep, and he sounded as if he'd hit the bottom of a whiskey bottle a few hours earlier.

"I had a dream."

"Crap." He grumbled. "Hold on, let me grab my notebook." I heard him yawn. "Okay, shoot."

"Blonde woman, sorry I couldn't see her face. I'd guess about five five. She was facedown in a pool of blood." I closed my eyes trying to remember the scene. "Something about her hair seemed familiar but I can't figure out what."

Kyle and I had been through this before. Sometimes the dreams were premonitions, like when our butler Mr. Peterson died. I saw him passed out in a chair with blood coming out of his eyes. I was five at the time and my parents wrote it off as a bad dream. Two weeks later Mr. Peterson died of a brain aneurysm. After that, they took the dreams more seriously.

As I grew older, the night terrors became more grisly. Sometimes I saw the murder as it happened, but from the killer's perspective. I could only see the victims and the scene around them, never who perpetrated the crime. I taught myself to take in the details of the scenes.

I met Kyle through my sister Alex a few years ago. A former FBI agent turned private investigator, he taught criminology at the University of Texas. She told him about the dreams one night when they were out on a date. Their romantic relationship didn't last long, but we all became friends. It was Kyle who encouraged me to look for clues in the dreams.

I pulled the sheets away from my legs and moved to the edge of the bed. "She's at a hotel. Sorry, motel. It's old, grungy. A-1 Motel. I saw it on a notepad on top of a busted lamp. Horrible bedspreads with diamond shapes. She's in a pool of blood. Naked."

I paused.

I could hear him scribbling on the notepad.

"I didn't get a name."

"Anything else?"

I closed my eyes again. "No. Uh, well, something weird happened at the end, but now I'm not so sure it was a part of the dream. It could have been something in my subconscious."

"Just tell me. It may be important."

"I heard a voice. It wasn't the victim's. It said, 'Soon, Guardian.'"

"Are you okay?" I could hear the concern in his voice.

I sighed. "It was a tough one, but I'm good."

He grunted. "I'll run this and see what turns up."

"Let me know. And I'll contact Jake and run it past him, too." The two men often worked cases together when our family was involved. Kyle never asked questions about how

Jake was able to get into every government database that existed, and Jake never wanted to know how Kyle was always able to come up with evidence the police missed. They were excellent at their jobs, and they had both served with the Marines so there was a certain kind of toughness about them. They also never minced words.

"Later." Kyle hung up.

I pushed the Off button. And rubbed my temples.

In addition to the nightmare, I had a killer migraine. That happened when I jumped more than once a day. I'd been all over the place last night, and now my body paid the price. The flulike symptoms meant electrolytes and enzymes were out of balance.

I'd only been asleep for three hours. As much as I wanted to roll over and pull the covers up, the real world beckoned. I needed to prepare for the meetings I had scheduled later in the day, and I had a feeling my demon problem was far from over.

My mother's French bulldog, Mo, whined from the ottoman. "Hey, fella. I'm guessing you need to go outside." I yawned. Whenever Mom was gone, Mo would stay with whoever was home. He didn't like to be alone. Except for the occasional drool puddle he left on the furniture, he was a pretty cool guy. He didn't lie and he didn't talk back. My sisters and I had long ago deemed Mo the perfect man. Well, man dog.

I wanted a cup of coffee laced with some of Mira's magic herbs. She'd prepared a mixture of herbs that eased the muscle aches and sent the migraines away.

Two cups of coffee and a blueberry muffin later, I was ready to face the world. My meetings were more than three hours away, which meant I had time to catch up on paperwork at the office. I poured another cup of coffee into a travel mug.

As I left the kitchen I bumped into Mrs. P. "Did you get a muffin? I baked them fresh this morning and put in extra berries just for you."

I squeezed her shoulder. "I did and they were incredible, as always."

She smiled. I loved the elderly woman. She reminded me of the church lady in those old *Saturday Night Live* sketches. I'd never eaten anything she'd cooked that I didn't like.

My phone rang. "I'll talk to you later." I waved good-bye to her and answered.

"Do you want the bad news or the sucky news first?" It was funny to hear Kyle say "sucky."

"Damn, that was fast. She's really dead, isn't she?" I knew the truth before he answered. Sometimes the dreams were premonitions, but lately I only saw the murders after the fact.

"Oh, yeah. ME says probably died around one this morning. Someone drugged her and then cut out her heart. They think it's a ritual killing, but aren't saying that on the record."

"Why would I see someone I didn't know? Doesn't make any sense." Most of the nightmares usually involved people I knew in some way. Or they might have been connected to my family, people who worked for us, or friends. Sometimes it took months to figure out how we knew them, but there was always some kind of connection.

"You did know her. It's Markie Stewart."

I stumbled and fell against the wall. "No. You have to be wrong. I was supposed to meet with her later this morning. It's not her, Kyle."

"I'm really sorry, Gillian. The police say she never made it home last night. She met friends after work at Le Vitrie for drinks and dinner. Looks like the assailant grabbed her in the parking lot. Her car is still at the restaurant. It's still early in the investigation, but the murder scene is set up to look random. I don't think it is. This isn't the first time this guy has killed and it's almost as if he staged the whole thing."

I only half listened. Markie had been a friend for years. She'd taken over her father's real estate company when he died. My family had been dealing with the Stewarts since long before she and I were even born.

We'd been chatting a lot the last month or so, and sort of renewed our friendship. Markie had a New York property that she thought might be good gallery space, and I'd been looking forward to seeing her.

Kyle's words finally penetrated my brain. "Wait, why don't you think it's random?"

"Too staged. I don't think she's the one who smashed the lamp. There are no prints at all, and he couldn't have wiped all the pieces clean. Nothing under her fingernails, even though they are broken, like she fought the attacker.

"Looks to me like he wanted us to think she struggled, but the drugs had been in her system for a while. My guess is he drugged her in the parking lot and then dumped her in a car or van. The motel is just outside the city off of Highway 35. Desk clerk says the guest paid by cash. Was wearing a hooded sweatshirt so not much on a description. Says the guy was tall, somewhere between thirty-five and fifty, and had light brown skin. That's it. It's a no-tell motel, so the people who work here don't pay much attention to the clientele."

I forced myself to walk to my room. I'd have to cancel the rest of my meetings. There was no way I could function. Death was a big part of my life, considering my job as a Guardian, but seldom did the subject involve my friends. The thought that it was Markie on that floor made my heart hurt, and I couldn't keep the tears from falling to my cheeks.

I popped open my laptop to send an e-mail to Georgia so she could deal with the appointments. "Her family is wealthy— do you think maybe it was a kidnapping gone wrong?" I held the cell between my shoulder and face so I could type. I clicked Send, and reached for a tissue.

"Nah. The detectives are running the scene through their database. They think it may be linked to a case in Seattle. But the place was wiped clean. This guy knew what he was doing."

I sat down in my desk chair and stared out the window. The sun brightened the landscape and the rich yellows and oranges of the changing leaves would have been a glorious sight, if I weren't mourning the loss of a friend. "How did you explain why you were there?"

"Didn't have to. Someone else called it in. Told them I heard it on the scanner and stopped by to see if they needed some help." That wasn't unusual. Kyle was a good profiler, as well as a detective, and consulted with several law enforcement agencies. It helped us that he was so well respected, because they never questioned why he always seemed to know so many details about the scenes. "So do you have any idea who might have wanted her dead?"

I bit my lip. "Not a clue. They have real estate holdings all over the world. Markie looked the part of a bubbleheaded blonde, but she had a wicked sense for business. Since she took over the company it's grown, but people love her. Kyle, I really hate this."

"I know." His voice was soft. He did understand. I never wanted these dreams, and they seemed to happen more often now.

I couldn't get the killer's voice out of my head. "Kyle?"

"Yeah?"

"The voice in my dream had an accent. I don't know what kind but it was European. He rolled his *r*'s. I'm usually good with that sort of thing, but I can't place it. Could have been Italian, French, or Spanish."

"Don't worry, Gillian. We'll find the guy. We always do." He hung up the phone.

I hugged my arms around my body and took a deep breath.

The killer wanted me to know he had the power to kill one of my friends. My heart ached for Markie and her family, but I was also worried about what this maniac might do next. He wasn't finished, I was certain about that.

I opened my cell phone. I needed my sisters and Bailey, and I needed them now.

CHAPTER

6

Alex arranged it so we could all meet at Club Zonk, one of the many nightclubs she owns. Our first pet was a lazy hound dog given to my dad by one of his friends, and we called him Zonk, because he never stayed awake for long. Years after he died we still used phrases like "I'm zonked." Or my favorite, "I'm zonkered."

The laid-back vibe of the place worked well in Austin. Every night the club was open there was a long line of patrons wanting to curl up on the large round leather sofas or dance on the dimly lit floor. Friends of Alex's showed up all the time to practice new songs in front of an audience. Blues, rock, country, it didn't matter. Club Zonk played a mixture of everything. Some of her clubs around the world were loud and wild discos, but Zonk lived up to its name. It was a quiet place to dance, drink, and hang out with friends.

The VIP area was upstairs behind what looked like a mirrored wall. On the other side of the glass was a comfy lounge with well-placed sofas, and curtained booths for privacy.

After letting the paparazzi snap a few photos I moved through the crowd at the door and into the VIP entrance. The area at the top of the stairs had been cordoned off with black rope and a "Private Party" sign.

Appetizer trays were tastefully displayed on a small buffet, and Alex sat in one of the large round booths talking on her cell. She motioned me toward her.

"Tell them I want them in cobalt or not at all, and if it's delayed one more day, I'll go to another supplier." She snapped the phone shut and reached up to grab my hand. "Are you okay? I'm so sorry about Markie."

I leaned down and kissed her cheek. "It's just wrong."

She nodded. "Patrick is bringing up a couple of pitchers of Matadors."

I raised an eyebrow.

"Hey, a little alcohol always helps the grieving process, and God knows we all need to relax a little. We've been under a lot of stress with the jobs, and *the jobs*." She rolled her eyes. "Now Markie. The universe is trying to tell us something, but I'm not sure what." She squeezed my hand. "Sit, Gilly. I'll grab us some food. Pele made us some of those stuffed mushrooms and some delectable crab bites."

She jumped up and walked to the buffet. With her long black hair pulled back in a tight ponytail, and wearing a halter top, rock star jeans, and Chloe boots, she looked like a young starlet. I was proud of her. Not only did she own some of the most successful clubs in the world, she fought some of the most difficult beings in the universe—dragons. She had the burns on her lower back and hip to prove it. The fire breathers had harder heads than demons and that was saying something.

The thought of demons made me wonder what Arath was doing. *Crap, that's totally random. Why the hell would I think about him?*

"Ohhh, who are you thinking about?" Alex put a platter of goodies in front of me. Before I could answer, Patrick, who managed the club when Alex was away, brought in the drinks.

"Hey, Gils, we haven't seen you in forever." I genuinely liked the guy. A former college football star, he had a tattooed head and bulging muscles. His Hell's Angel biker look was deceiving. The man had a good mind for business, and kept things running smoothly so Alex could concentrate on opening new clubs. Patrick was also one hell of a bartender. She had a knack for finding the right people for the right job.

He poured me a Matador and I sipped the Red Bull, limeade, Triple Sec, and tequila concoction. "Whew, that is some good stuff." I smiled at him.

He winked at me. "A couple of those and all your troubles will melt away."

I wish.

"Thanks for this, and tell Pele his crab bites are mind-blowing."

Patrick laughed. "No way. The chef's big head barely fits in the kitchen as it is. If I tell him you like it, he'll be whipping up something else for you to try, and our guests will go hungry tonight."

Alex sat back in the booth.

Patrick picked up the tray that had held the drinks. "You guys need anything, just call me downstairs."

Claire and Bailey passed him on the way in, and they stopped to say hi before heading over. Bailey was in jeans and vintage tee. He must have been working, because his curls were a mess. He had two pencils stuck behind his right ear as if he'd forgotten about the first one he put there.

Claire wore a minidress made out of silky yellow material that went fabulously with her blonde curls.

I smiled at them both. "I love you guys." They group-hugged me.

"Please, she was our friend, too," Bailey said. "Tell me we're going after the bastard who killed her."

"Of course we are," Mira said behind him. Her red curls framed her face, and she wore jeans with a green V-neck T-shirt and black leather jacket. "He's going to pay for messing with a friend of ours. So tell us the details, Gilly."

Alex poured everyone drinks and I shared everything Kyle had told me. I also explained about the dream, and the voice I'd heard.

"Do any of you know of who would want to hurt her?"

A chorus of "no" circled the table.

I blew out a breath. "I have no idea what's going on in the universe. Murder never happens at a good time, but I'm dealing with a hardheaded demon king. And I have a sense that things are going to get bad very fast. I can't explain it. Something doesn't feel right."

"I don't know if it's related, but I haven't had a day or night off in weeks," Alex admitted. "The dragons are causing me extreme burnout. Pun intended." She smirked. "I don't know why but there are more jumpers than ever and I can't tell you how many I've had to haul back to the other side. It's almost like they are afraid. What I don't get is why they would jump to this world, when they know we're going to kill them or take them back. Doesn't make any sense."

Claire took a sip of her drink and pursed her lips. "Whew. That's strong. I'm with you, Al. I've spent more time in the water than on land the last few days. I had one angry water pony who tried to take down a shrimp boat. That was not an easy thing to explain to the fishermen. I finally convinced them that they'd seen a genetically modified whale. Thank God, no one took pictures. The thing caused a huge dent in the bow of the ship, but they didn't take on any water."

Bailey sat back. "How about you, Mira?" He looked at her as if he knew something the rest of us didn't.

She gave him a withering stare, and he only smiled. "Fine. I was attacked by a group of Fae. Last night, when I was in

Panama meeting with a pharmaceutical company rep about some new products. When we stepped out onto the street we were jumped by a group of seven-foot, blonde-headed fairies. One of them had the nerve to pull a knife. I saw it coming, but he took a chunk out of me when I tried to push the rep out of the way." She showed us the bandage on her shoulder. "I was able to take care of them and shoved them through a portal. Scary part is, they didn't show up on the radar."

"Same here." Claire raised a hand. "One of our guys heard about a ship in distress and I jumped to check it out."

I chewed on my lip. "How the hell is that happening? We have trackers on every portal on Earth. There's no way they can get through."

"They can if new portals are being opened," Bailey chimed in.

"But the treaties." Alex coughed. "It isn't possible."

"Yeah, it is. All it takes is a couple of worlds deciding they don't want to honor the treaties anymore, and boom, we have a war on our hands." Bailey crossed his arms against his chest and frowned. His brilliant mind was already at work coming up with solutions. That's what he did best. That and design cool weapons.

"Do you think that's what Mom and Aunt Juliet are doing at the high council meeting?" Claire pulled her hair behind her ears. She was more sensitive to change than the rest of us, but she was still queen when it came to killing water-related bad guys.

I shrugged. "Have any of you heard from her?"

There was another chorus of "no."

"That's weird. Usually she'd tell at least one of us." I picked up my cell phone and dialed Jake. He would know where Mom was.

He answered on the first ring. "I'm sorry about Miss Stewart. I know she was a friend." Jake sounded sincere but distracted.

"Thank you. Is something wrong?"

"Marshall says six jumpers landed in." He paused for a moment. "Rome. Right in the middle of Vatican City."

"Oh, hell. I'm on my way." I hung up the phone and pushed Bailey out of the booth so I could stand up. Before I could say anything, cell phones rang all around. My sisters rolled their eyes.

There wasn't time to talk, but it would be a long night for the Caruthers sisters. Alex ran for her office. "I've got two sabers and three of Bailey's new guns in here." She also had an ax, which I borrowed along with a sword. Demon heads can be tough to cut off.

"Let's catch up later. This is beyond weird. Thanks, you guys, for being here tonight. It meant a lot." I waved.

Claire blew me a kiss and then picked up one of Bailey's guns. I heard her say, "Show me how this puppy works," to Bailey as I touched my tattoos together and teleported away.

Thirty seconds later I landed on my butt in front of St. Peter's Basilica. I'd been here many times before, so I recognized it instantly. "What is it with these guys and holy places?" I followed the screams. Several priests ran from a small building to the left.

Damn. I booked it to the door, which led to a small meeting room. It was empty, but I saw another door had been busted that opened into a large dining room with tables.

What the hell are those?

There were three winged demons flying around the room in circles.

"Come on, you big idiots, come and get me." I swung the ax behind my back so they couldn't see it and ran as fast as I could.

They acted as guards keeping me from the door, but wouldn't come near enough for me to kill them. If I had brought one of the guns, I could have picked them off and been done with it. As I moved closer to the door where the other demons had gone, the three winged monsters dove for me. Claws out and teeth bared, the first swooped low and caught me from behind. He pulled me up by the hair.

My skull felt like it split in two as I brought the ax up with my right arm and sliced a clean cut in the creature's neck. I knew I'd hit my target when it screeched and green goo dropped on my head and my boots. Luckily I was only a few feet off the ground when it dropped me, so I didn't have far to fall.

I heard something human behind me and swung around. One of the priests had returned and he held a rosary as he prayed.

"Father, get out of here. These things will kill you."

"No. I saw you come in to fight the hell spawn. I will not leave you alone." He was young, and probably idealistic, but I didn't have time to argue with him. Unless that rosary had blades on it, I wasn't sure it would do him much good against the crazy birds. But I never questioned a person's faith.

Another of the winged monsters dipped down and tried to pry the ax away with its claws. It had ahold of my wrist, and its claws ripped the flesh from my bones. I used my left hand to grab the saber from where I'd stuck it in my back belt. Swinging my arm up, I drove the sharp point through the head. The damn thing wouldn't let go of my wrist even in death. I sliced away the claw still attached to me.

"Watch out!" the priest screamed as the last of the creatures swooped down. Not sure where its heart was, I pierced the chest with the saber and then brought the ax up in my other hand. There was so much blood I couldn't see where the ax began and my hand ended. I used what strength I had left in it to slice upward and hit some kind of artery. The thing fell to the floor screeching.

"Father, I have to go after the others. Please, for both of our sakes, don't follow me. I can't protect us both. Keep everyone out of here until I can clean up this mess."

He stared at me for a moment.

I shrugged. It was never easy explaining something most humans had no idea existed. "I know. Demon spawn on Earth would freak people out. So let's keep this between you and me. The rest of those guys running for their lives just wouldn't understand. I appreciate your bravery, but we have to keep these things quiet. Okay? I promise I'll be back in a few minutes. This is what I do."

I'm not sure if he believed me, but he nodded.

I took off down another long hallway.

A big light flashed at the end of the hall. "No!" I ran as fast as I could but I was too late. The demons had used a temporary portal to get out of the room. The remains of a steel door was all that was left. Whatever had been in the room was now gone. All that was left was a marble slab and several smashed safe-deposit boxes. Or at least that was what it looked like. It took me a minute to realize it was a room-sized safe. "This isn't good."

I raced back to the dining area. "Father, I need a couple of trash bags, and can you tell me what was in the last room on the right? The one with the bank vault inside?"

"Was?" His eyes teared. "No, they couldn't have taken it all. That is the papal treasury. Priceless jewels and artifacts from centuries were stored there. Even some artwork in the larger boxes."

Oh, damn. "You'll need to find out what they took. Not all of the boxes were smashed so it's possible they were after something specific." I pulled out a business card from the back pocket of my jeans. "When you have a good accounting of what's gone, call this number and ask for Jake. He knows how to get in touch with me. I promise I'll do my best to get your treasure back, but first I need those trash bags."

He ran behind the counter where a buffet had been set out. "I do not have bags but I have this." He wheeled out a large garbage can.

I smiled at him. "That will do. I hear sirens. Can you keep them away for a few moments?" I threw the three demons in the can with my left hand. The right was almost useless now. The demon poison had begun to shrivel the skin. It burned like hell, but I didn't have time to worry about war wounds. I had to get the creatures out of there before the police showed up.

"What do I say?" He turned back to stare at me.

"The truth, Father, that thieves stole the treasure. If I find it, I promise to return it."

"May I ask you something?"

"Sure."

"Are you Gillian Caruthers?" That was the tough part about having to deal with humans on the job. On occasion we had to send in a mage to clear memories or change things a bit. I didn't think we'd have to do that here.

I gave him my best fake chuckle. "People say I look like her all the time. I'm flattered. I think she's kind of pretty." *You are so going to hell, Gilly girl.*

The look in his eye told me he knew I'd lied. He made the sign of the cross in front of him. "Whoever you are, God be with you." He couldn't be much older than me, but there was wisdom in those eyes. I knew he'd handle the situation.

As he turned to follow my orders I pulled one of the watches from my pocket. I pushed the button and grabbed hold of the trash can.

Arath had some explaining to do.

CHAPTER

7

"What the hell are these things? And if you say 'demons,' I'll kill you."

Arath met me at the door. "Threatening a demon king is never wise, Guardian. You are injured." He pointed to my right hand.

"Yeah. I'm not really interested in the obvious right now. Are you going to tell me what these things are? I've seen a lot of demons, studied even more, but I've never seen anything that looked like this." I lifted the lid of the can. The stench, a cross between rotten eggs and something Mo the bulldog threw up on my rug a few weeks ago, made the bile rise in my stomach.

"Shoreh. They are pets of the Nira clan. Where did you find them?" He lifted one out of the can and examined it.

"They were in one of our holiest places, guarding the door while someone else stole priceless antiquities. I didn't actually see your people do the deed, but since these are demon pets, and our security team saw the jumpers, they must've had something to do with it."

"I will order Comdar, the head of the clan here. He is no thief, so I am certain he will have an explanation." He threw the dead batlike creature back in the can. *"Rockschlt!"* He roared the word and demons suddenly appeared from the doorways, At least thirty of them filled the hall. "Bring Comdar to me!" The demon horde bowed and fled through the front hallway.

"Before you leave, let me heal your injuries." He pointed to the hand that still held the ax. I wasn't sure I could let go of the weapon since the blood had dried and it now felt permanently attached.

"I don't have any plans to leave." I stood just to the right of the front door. "I want the antiquities back. They are very important to a certain religion, and I promised to bring them back." I wasn't Catholic, but had a feeling lying to a priest meant bad karma any way you looked at it.

"Demon hunter, you are in no shape to argue with me. I will heal your hand, and you will return home to rest. It may be several days before Comdar arrives. His clan lives underground in the Blashen Forest."

"Well, since you're the almighty demon king, then you should be able to know exactly where they are and teleport them here. Or they can teleport themselves. They certainly had no problem making it out of that vault before I could get to them."

He grunted. "I am flattered that you think me so powerful I could pick someone off of the planet and bring them to me, but you are wrong. Let me heal your hand. We will discuss Comdar later." He turned and walked behind one of the tapestries.

I stood for a moment. He hadn't even asked if I'd follow him, but if he could heal some of the damage to my hand it was worth swallowing any pride I had left. My head was going numb from the poisoned demon claws, and I couldn't actually feel my arm, which, when I saw it, was probably a good thing.

Behind the tapestry was a large room with several more doors. The one in the center was open so I assumed that was where he'd gone.

On the other side of the archway was a big surprise. A large kitchen with herbs on shelves, a sink, and several gas burners. It could have been a kitchen back home.

Arath had a large mortar and pestle and was throwing herbs from the various containers into it and smashing them to bits.

"Put down the weapon. I will not harm you." He concentrated on his mixture.

I tried to open my hand to drop the weapon but it wouldn't work. "I can't."

He poured some liquid into a blue glass bottle and added the herbs. After shaking the concoction, he set it on the counter.

"Come here." He met me at the sink. It was carved out of the same stone as the countertop and had the look of granite. Using the spray from the water he washed some of the blood off my arm. His hand rested on my shoulder and a heat spread down to my wrist.

"Yikes." I growled as the feeling returned to my extremity. "I mean thanks." I said the words through clenched teeth.

"The pain will pass. You've sustained a great deal of damage from the poison."

When my hand finally relaxed, the ax clattered against the stone. It stung like crazy, as if tiny fire ants were chewing their way out of my skin. I bit the inside of my lip to keep from screaming.

"It would not shame you to cry." He moved his glowing touch down to my hand. It still burned, but it wasn't as bad.

"I don't cry." I closed my eyes and tried to will the pain away. Guardians never showed weakness. We didn't cry, especially when we were in pain. It was a state of mind. If I made myself believe it didn't hurt, the pain would stop.

His tender hands moved over the skin of my wrist and thankfully the burning became a light tingle. I opened one eye to see what had happened, surprised to see the skin healing.

"Jeez, you're powerful."

"We are not done. Your skin lacks color. You must sit."

I did feel woozy. He lifted me with one hand around my waist and put me on the counter. "The poison is attacking your nervous system. Guardians are made stronger than humans;

73

otherwise, you would be dead." He handed me the bottle. "Drink this."

Dead? I didn't feel so great, but dead? I lifted the bottle to my mouth. It didn't smell much better than the rotting demons in the trash can.

"You must drink it now." He pushed it to my lips again.

I drank it in two gulps. "Ack. Sorry, but that's nasty."

"It will work, but it takes time. You must rest."

I nodded. "How did you learn this? I mean, I saw your power to heal at the amusement park, but you're as good as my mom with the herbs."

"My father made certain that I was trained in all matters of magic and healing so that I could face the most formidable of foes. I demand that you rest, Guardian. Your body cannot heal if you continue to push."

"Before I do that, can you do something about these scratches on the back of my head?" I parted my hair so he could see.

"*Mesht.*" I didn't know the word, but I understood its meaning. "You are the one who is powerful. This close to the human brain, you are lucky you are not paralyzed."

His hands moved over my head gently. He pushed tiny strands of hair back from my forehead.

I inhaled his scent, a mixture of musk and cloves. His eyes held concern, and something happened in that moment. I didn't see him just as the demon king, I saw him as a man.

He's not a man. Get it together, Gillian. He's a demon.

Arath pulled back and looked at me as if he knew what I'd been thinking.

The burning ants took over the top of my scalp. I knew what to expect so I didn't groan this time, but when his hand reached the back of my neck the pain dissipated.

Unfortunately, so did any energy I had left. He caught me as I tumbled off the counter, and carried me in his arms like a baby.

"Home," I managed to whisper.

"Soon," he said as he touched my cheek.

I wished he didn't smell so good.

CHAPTER

8

It was noon the next day before my eyes even thought about opening. I tested a quick blink, surprised there were no ill effects from the previous night.

There was just one problem. I didn't remember getting to my room.

"The demon king brought you home." The simple statement sounded like an insult coming from my mother. I didn't need to see her to know she wasn't happy with me. She pulled the curtains back and I blinked against the light.

I opened my mouth to explain. She held up a hand.

"I'm not angry, child. Arath told Jake that your strength and sheer willpower were what kept you alive." Some mothers might have been weeping with joy that their child had survived. Not mine.

Oh, she loved me and was glad I was alive, but there was no doubt she was disappointed in me. Rule number two in the Guardian's handbook is to never show weakness. The fact that the demon king had had to save my life was a big no-no.

"I'm sorry." I didn't know what else to say. It sounded lame even to me. "I know I've disappointed you."

Mom sat on the edge of the bed and pursed her lips. She was dressed in a long red skirt with a matching sweater and boots. She looked as though she'd just stepped out of a Carolina Herrera store. Prim and proper, with a simple gold chain at her neck and the diamond studs she never took out of her ears. My dad had given them to her on their twenty-fifth wedding anniversary, just two years before he died. Her white-blonde hair was held by a clip at the base of her neck. She didn't look like a powerful mage. It was a part of her deception.

"On the contrary. It seems you have a fan in the demon king. Jake said Arath was quite worried about you. He stayed for several minutes to make sure the men followed his instructions explicitly. Including telling Jake to call me."

She took my hand in hers. "The healers tell me that whatever magic he used on you saved your life. He's quite powerful."

I crossed my legs under the sheet. "I've never come across anyone like him. Do you know about him?"

She dropped my hand and stood. "If you're asking if I know

about his mother and father, the answer is yes." Her steel gray eyes stared at me. "I assume you've discovered the truth about his parents, or at least part of it." She glanced down at her watch. "I don't have time to explain, but I'd appreciate it if you could keep this quiet for now. There are circumstances." She sighed. "It's complicated. I have to go."

I knew a brush-off when I heard one, but I had to know the truth. "Mom, how could she leave her children behind? It doesn't sound like something Aunt Juliet would do."

Her hand stilled on the door. "Gillian, she didn't *leave* her children. She thinks they are dead. There has been a shift in the universe and problems with the treaties. We're dealing with some very dark magic, and all hell is about to break loose. I don't use that phrase lightly. I don't have time to discuss King Arath's lineage right now."

My mother never did anything lightly. If she was worried, things were much worse than I could ever imagine. I moved my legs to the side of the bed. "What do you mean?"

"There was a reason why you girls were kept so busy last night. They wanted you distracted. Someone set a plan in motion that could destroy our world and several others. It's going to take all of us working together to keep the peace."

She reached the door and turned back. "And, Gillian, I'm sorry about your friend Markie. Jake told me what happened. I've given Jake some of my theories. I think someone may be trying to distract you in a horrific way. They want to catch you off guard and drive you away from your purpose. It's possible we are on the precipice of war. Do you understand what I'm saying?"

I did. Be focused and concentrate on what is most important. One of the many lessons she'd drummed into our heads. If the treaties were dissolved it wouldn't cause problems just for Earth; other worlds could also be destroyed. It was the Guardian Keys' duty to make sure that didn't happen.

Even if the end of the world might be on the way, I still had work to do. Our main offices were downtown, and if I had to be gone for a few days it was always good to go in even for a short time to show my face.

I signed papers and did about four weeks' worth of work in three hours. I'm lucky that my assistant, Georgia, is incredibly good at her job and mine. She makes it easy on me. Thanks to her I was able to catch up and get ahead. She was one of the few people at Caruthers Corp. who knew about both sides of my life.

I also had a press conference scheduled with Roland Falk, the owner of one of the largest art supply companies in the world. He was one of the major contributors to our Arts in Schools program, and he would be one of several people honored at the big arts ball. Even though I didn't really have time, the conference would work to my benefit.

The press would see me in my capacity as CEO and fundraiser, and the appearance would make it look like I was at the office working hard. It also pleased Roland, which meant big bucks for our program, something dear to my heart.

Caruthers Corp. had several floors and we kept a large conference room on the first floor for events like this. Our publicity coordinator, Sharron, introduced me, and then I talked about Roland and his many contributions to the cause. He gave about a five-minute speech, and then we took questions.

A handsome man, Roland didn't look anywhere near his sixty years of age. He'd been friends with my parents for as long as I could remember. When my father died, he was there for all of us. I thought maybe at some point he and my mom might date, but they never had anything but a casual dinner together once a month or so at the club.

All went according to plan with the press until Franklin Conrad from WJLP radio asked, "Ms. Caruthers, would you like to comment on your involvement with the recent murder of Markie Stewart? Is it true she had an affair with your boyfriend, Emilio? A source of mine says she bought several of his paintings in the last few weeks."

A solid left punch to the chin would have hurt less. Tears burned the corners of my eyes. I put on the biggest fake smile I had and killed the reporter with kindness. "We are here to talk about Arts in Schools, a cause that my lovely friend Markie Stewart was actively involved in. She was a wonderful and talented businesswoman, and one of my dearest friends. Her love of art was evident by the huge collection she amassed over the years. Many of the pieces I advised her on were purchased through my galleries. As we mentioned in the release, she is one of the people, along with Roland, whom we will honor at the ball."

Sharron, bless her, leaned into the microphone. "That's all we have time for today. We have copies of the release on the table by the door."

I'd always been envious of Sharron's toasted almond skin, but I also admired her ability to do her job. She never let me down, especially in tough situations like this.

She turned off the mike and squeezed my hand. "He's an ass," she whispered. "I'll take care of it."

"Thanks." I squeezed back.

Roland put a hand on my shoulder. "Let's get you back to your office. William?" He pointed to his bodyguard, a bald Latino man who was about the same size as Arath, only much wider. "Please help Ms. Caruthers to her office."

The reporters, as stunned as I was by the turn of events, fired off questions as William cut a path through them. Roland was on one side of me, Sharron on the other, and Georgia brought up the rear.

"I'll notify security about what happened, and Sharron will send out a release to employees that they are not to discuss anything to do with Ms. Stewart's death," Georgia said once we made it into the elevator.

"The gall of the man, trying to tie you to the murder." Roland huffed in disgust. "The media can be a useful tool, but it took everything I had not to punch him as we walked by."

That made me smile. "Thank you, Roland. Thanks to all of you for helping me. It's unfortunate that had to happen." I tried to be professional, but inside I couldn't help wondering what the reporter meant. Had Emilio and Markie been seen together? I advised her on all of her art buys and kept an extensive inventory of her collections. As far as I knew, she'd never purchased any of Emilio's art.

When the doors opened, I stepped out with Sharron and Georgia, while Roland and William stayed behind to go back down. "You know there's a secret entrance to the garage on the third floor?"

Roland took my hand in his. "Yes, love, but I'll not be hiding away in secret. We are doing good work, and I'm not going to let some nasty reporter keep us from doing that. I'll leave through the front door, thank you." He squeezed my hand and then waved good-bye.

Back in my office I called Kyle. He'd already seen the press conference, which had been carried live by several local stations. That's why we'd done it at five.

"Do you know what he was talking about?" Kyle answered the phone with a question.

"No. Not a clue. I mean, they'd met through dinners with me, but I don't know what that guy meant. Markie isn't the kind of woman to have affairs with her friends' boyfriends. She was a flirt, but a straight-up human being." I sat down at my desk and turned to look out at the sun dipping behind the build-ings downtown. "You know, at first when he said that about my involvement I panicked for a few seconds and thought he meant the dream. Freaked me out in a big way."

"Well, you handled it with your usual professionalism. I promise to check into it right away. If something was going on, I'll have an answer for you in a few hours."

I sighed. "If they had an affair, I'm not sure I want to know."

"I hear ya. Listen, Jake mentioned you guys are having some trouble with some kind of universal shifts. I don't prom-ise to know what the hell that is, but I do know it's creating problems for you and your sisters. So as hard as it might be, you concentrate on the saving-the-world stuff, and I'll handle the earthbound crap."

I blew out a breath. "Thanks, Kyle."

After hanging up, I stretched my arms above my head, will-ing the tension away. I noticed Georgia standing in the door-way. She had a strange expression.

"What is it?"

"There's a—Mr. Arath to see you. Security in the lobby says he's very insistent. Told them that he doesn't need an appointment"—she cleared her throat—"and that it's most urgent."

Oh, my God. I jumped up. The last thing I needed was a demon king running around the building with reporters everywhere. "Tell them to send him up in the private elevator, and hold my calls, please." The last bit came out as a squeak and I coughed to cover my nervousness.

She nodded.

I made myself stop biting the inside of my lip.

A few minutes later Georgia escorted Arath into my office. Dressed in what looked like a Savile Row suit, he was so big, he seemed to fill every inch of the room.

"Thank you, Georgia." I waited for her to close the door, then turned to address Arath. "You can't just show up at my workplace whenever you want." I gritted my teeth. "You shouldn't be here at all. There are news reporters everywhere—if one of them had seen you—" I threw my hands up in the air. "Why can't you understand that demons are not welcome here?"

"I do understand how your world feels about my people." He sat down in one of the cushy chairs opposite my desk, the same one Bailey had occupied a few nights ago. "I need to speak with your mother, but I'm told she is on council business. So I came to speak to the Guardian instead."

I closed my eyes for a moment, trying to calm down. "We have strict procedures for this sort of thing. If you need me, you contact Jake. I could have been in Maunra in a matter of minutes."

"This is true"—he nodded—"but you may have not been safe."

I pushed a hand through my hair. "Arath, why are you here?" Was he perhaps one of the distractions Mom had warned me about? Maybe he was in with whoever it was that caused the trouble.

"I wish you no harm, only to tell you that traveling through the portals can be dangerous for all of the Guardians. There is an evil magic at work, and it has unbalanced the universe. It is a perverse magic that can do great injury should you try to pass through it."

I sat, well, actually sort of fell, back into my chair. "Do you know who is behind the magic?"

"No, but it grows quickly in strength. When the Guardians travel to other worlds, they—you—must make certain the portals have not been tainted by the darkness."

I leaned forward with my elbows on the desk. "I don't mean to seem ungrateful, but couldn't you have sent us a message?"

"It is important that you understand the magnitude of what has happened. The universe changes as we speak."

Taking a slow breath, I rose. "Thank you. I will warn my sisters and get a message to my mother and the council. I will say that my mother mentioned to me earlier that they are aware of the magic, though they perhaps don't know about the latest development with the portals. I'm sure they'll be appreciative of your help."

He stood, and I once again noticed the impeccable fit of the suit, and the white shirt beneath.

"I'll escort you to a safe place where you can open a portal, but I have a quick question."

"Yes?"

"Where did you get that suit? It fits as if it were tailor-made for you." A couple nights earlier, he looked like a pirate, but today he had the air of royalty. Technically, that was exactly what he was.

"It was. I have studied your world a great deal, and knew I must try to fit in with the humans here. The suit was given to me and made to fit by one of my people who trades with other worlds."

"Huh." Well, okay then.

As we passed through the office, several of the employees pretended they didn't notice Arath, but he was hard to miss. At the outside of the cubicles, I said rather loudly, "Mr. Arath, thank you so much for coming today. I'm looking forward to doing business with you." I hoped that would help quell any gossip, but I doubted it.

I guided him down the hall to the men's restroom. "This is the safest place for you to, um, go." That didn't come out quite the way I'd planned. "Just make sure that no one is in the stalls before you teleport. And please, the next time you feel it necessary"—I held up a hand—"no matter how important the message, please contact us first. It just makes life easier on everyone."

After staring at me for a moment, he made a slight bow and said, "Be well, Guardian." Then he stepped through the door to the men's room.

I leaned against the wall for a minute, thinking about what

he'd said. The universe had shifted. We'd all felt it the last few days. The jumpers had been no accident.

The first order of business was to call my family. I couldn't risk someone being hurt in one of the tainted portals.

"You should go home and get some rest." It was several hours later and Georgia stood in the doorway.

"I don't know about resting, but I think I need a change of scenery. If you need me, I'm just a phone call away. And I hate to ask you, but do your best to make it look like I'm here the next few days. You know what happens when they"— I waved a hand toward the outside office—"think the cat's away."

Georgia smiled. "No problem, boss." She might be tiny at around four feet eleven, but no one ever messed with her. She could be a tyrant if necessary, and she knew how to run the corporation as well as I did. Even my mother was impressed by her. That meant something.

She handed me a handful of messages. "He's called seventy-two times in the last twenty-four hours. I kid you not. Can I hire someone to rough him up?"

Emilio. It seemed like so long ago, but in actuality it had only been a few days since I last saw him. Could he have had something to do with Markie's death? "Nah. I like that he's suffering, but you do have my permission to block his calls.

That's what I did on the cell. Okay. Again, if you need me, don't be afraid to—"

"Be careful saving the world," she interrupted.

I laughed. "Thanks for being the best right-hand chick a girl could ever have."

"Ah, go on. You'll make me cry and my mascara will be on my chin." She waved me away.

CHAPTER

9

From the car I scheduled a meeting with my sensei. Each of us had a multitude of trainers at our disposal at all times. If the end of the world was on the way, I needed to be centered, focused, and Master Kanashi was the one person I could count on for that.

Twenty minutes later I was dressed in black leggings and a tank. We have three mirrored studios in the house, and a full gym we shared with employees. It allowed all of us to train at the same time if necessary. Sometimes we'd spar together, depending on where we were and what we needed.

As Guardians we had to keep our mental and physical capabilities at their peak at all times. We trained an average of four days a week. Wing chun, savate, Shaolin kung fu, jujitsu, aikido, muay Thai, and eskrima are just a few of the martial arts I've studied. I work out with weights some, though with my strength it's not really necessary, and I run to keep my heart clear of gunk. Never knowing what kind of enemy we might face meant we had to be proficient in many things.

From the time we could stand, we worked with our mother and with masters of all the martial arts. It has always been a part of our lives.

I'd been lax the last few days; almost dying and chasing demons will do that to a girl. But my body told me it needed this.

In the studio Master Kanashi waited. As I entered I bowed, to show her respect. She did the same.

I'd had several teachers over the years, but Master K was the best. Formally trained in twelve martial arts, she also knew how to fight dirty. That came in handy with a Guardian's job. She was awesome with weapons, and at the same time had taught me how to meditate and find my center.

"Sensei, thank you for being here on such short notice."

Nodding my way, she closed her eyes and put her hands in a prayer position. Her short black hair had been spiked with blue tips. She grabbed her sword from the harness on her back. At one time, she had been an Army Ranger and had more scars than me and my sisters combined, including one where her throat had been slit from ear to ear.

I opened my bag and pulled out my saber. I'm not sure how

she always knew what I needed but she always did. I'd never asked because she couldn't speak.

We sparred with the swords for half an hour, then I finally pulled back. I had to catch my breath.

She cocked her head.

"I know, no excuses, but I almost died last night. I think my stamina may be a little low."

Her left eyebrow raised, and I knew she wanted to continue.

Half a bottle of water later, I took a deep breath. She moved into tae kwon do and then we beat the crap out of some punching bags. My muscles were loose and by the end I had worked out much of the tension and anger from the last few days. I will admit to seeing Emilio's face on the bag—it's a good thing he was nowhere close.

At the end of every workout we do seated meditation. Master K lit a candle and I dimmed the lights in the studio. Meditation isn't always easy for me, and it helped me sometimes to concentrate on the flame.

After a bit of "skull cleansing"—staccato breathing that aids relaxation—my shoulders dropped about another inch. My breathing deepened as I stared at the flame. It took almost ten minutes but eventually I could see nothing but white light healing my body and renewing my energy.

I was about to blow out the flame, which signals the end of our session, when a vision flashed before my eyes. A man facedown on a rug. I reached out and caught Master Kanashi's hand. "I need paper and pen," I whispered. She didn't question me but moved away, and a few seconds later she put the pen and a small notebook in my hand.

I concentrated on the vision. He had curly red hair and wore a white long-sleeved dress shirt. The slacks were gray with a black belt. He looked like he was sleeping, except there was a pool of blood, and his right arm was broken backward. His left leg was twisted and crushed, from the look of it.

Look for the details. I tried to pull back on the vision to see what kind of room he was in. The floor, a dark wood, was highly polished. A hat stand was to the left and a side table with a mirror stood against the wall. Whoever attacked him must have done it as he entered. His soft leather briefcase had spilled its contents; papers were strewn everywhere.

There were two arched entries, one off to the right and the other straight ahead. The walls were a soft blue. I looked down at the welcome mat. It read, "Welcome to the Arnolds."

No. My teeth clenched. I looked back at the body. *Red hair.* My heart thumped so loudly I had to take another breath to calm myself. I knew it was Reuben Arnold. He'd been our IT manager at Caruthers Corp. for three years. There wasn't a computer problem the man couldn't figure out.

My family trusted him so much that he was one of the few Caruthers Corp. employees we integrated into our operation here at the estate. He'd implemented many of Bailey's inventions to make all of our lives easier.

I made another quick survey of the room. As I did, I made a motion with my hand to indicate I needed my cell phone.

Kanashi moved to get what I needed. I continued to make notes on the paper without looking. This time there was no voice, but I had no doubt we were dealing with the same killer. It was more of a sense of the scene than anything.

I closed my eyes and the scene vanished. I pushed the speed dial.

"Yeah." Kyle's gruff tone answered. "I'm working on your Emilio angle. Don't have anything yet."

"There's been another murder."

"Damn. Give me the details."

Master K sat down in front of me again, giving me support. I could tell she was shocked, and there wasn't much that surprised her.

I gave Kyle the information and my voice cracked when I mentioned it was Reuben.

"I'm sorry, Gillian. There just aren't words. Look, the killer's escalating and trying to get closer to you. Do you know of anyone who wants to hurt you?"

A few hundred demon families, but I couldn't say that. "I'm sorry but I really don't. I do know it's the same person as Markie's killer, but I don't have any way of proving it." I checked my notes to make sure I hadn't missed anything.

"Your instincts are almost always on target. I'll make some calls and get back to you. If you remember anything else call me."

He hung up.

I chewed on my lip and sniffled.

Master K's arm moved around my shoulders and gave me a squeeze.

I patted her hand. "Thanks. I guess I should explain."

She shrugged her shoulders, as if to say I could talk if I wanted or not. I didn't normally share information unless I absolutely had to, but it felt right to tell her.

"I get these dreams, more nightmares really than anything. Sometimes they're premonitions, other times it's after the fact of a violent crime. This is the first time I've had one awake, which is beyond weird. I know this probably all sounds crazy."

Master Kanashi's eyes held understanding. She put her hands in the prayer position.

"I think you're right; it was when I was most relaxed that it happened. I'm sorry about the gruesome details. Thank you for helping me."

She gave me a short smile, something I'd never seen on her face, and her eyebrows went up. As an Army Ranger she'd seen her share of gore.

"I guess you've pretty much seen it all, but it's tough when it's someone you know and respect." I sighed. "He was a really good man."

There was a knock on the door.

I jumped up to open it. "Yes."

Jake stood on the other side. "We've got..." He looked past

me and saw Master K. "...A situation that needs your immediate attention."

I bowed to my sensei. "Thanks again."

"Tell me what we've got," I said as Jake and I ran for the control room.

CHAPTER

10

So many demons, so little time. My mother and Arath hadn't lied about something being amiss in the universe. Our entire family was on high alert. The idea that someone might be keeping us busy and distracted hadn't escaped any of us. It wasn't just the murders, everything was nuts.

I'd been back at the house for twenty minutes and listened as my sisters reported in. Mystical and demonic creatures, all of which seemed to be after some sort of treasure, were over-running Earth.

I'd just defeated six Morgre demons. They were nasty, toxic creatures that looked like a cross between a kangaroo with horns, and a man. I discovered the power of their legs when my roundhouse kick missed and I took a hit to the ribs.

I didn't hit the ground but I did stumble. I knew the ribs on my right side were probably broken, because it hurt like hell to breathe. That made me angry. I'd already taken down three of the monsters and I turned my fury on the others.

They circled me, expecting me to jump at any second and strike. Staying in a crouching position, I used my saber to take out their big kangaroo ankles in one hard-core hit. My shoulders and arms shook with the effort, but it worked. They all three fell back helpless without the use of their feet for balance. After a quick decapitation their bodies became a big pile of black ash. That happened with certain demons, and it made cleanup a lot easier.

This had been my third round with a gang of demons. The first was at a museum in Florence, and the second on a deserted street in Cairo. There were several trinket shops surrounding the area, which made me wonder if these demons had also been after some sort of treasure. The Morgres had been just outside a church in Paris where jewels of former kings and queens were stored in crypts below.

"Why can't we just shut down the damn portals?" I questioned Jake as I watched the blips disappear on the monitors. We were in the control room and the blips had finally slowed down.

Before he could answer, Mira walked in. "Black magic. Mom and your demon king were right. I helped Alex close down hers, and with our help we shut down Claire's. Something is definitely wrong. I'm going to need your help and probably Mom or Aunt Juliet to close mine. We couldn't do it ourselves."

"We sent an electronic pulse, which usually shuts down everything immediately, but it bounced back," added Jake. Thanks to Bailey we'd discovered that a combo of science and magic sometimes tilted the universe in our favor. Bailey had developed the pulse a few years ago, when we'd had trouble with one of the worlds breaking its treaty. "The good news is the jumpers have slowed down."

I paced behind the control panels. The security directors were talking through their comms. All of them were nervous, and I didn't blame them. They were human, and though most of them had been with us several years, none of us had ever seen anything like this.

"At least they aren't attacking," said Mira. She had a large cut on her shoulder. "From what I heard from Alex and Claire, there were three or four jumpers who were after some kind of treasure."

"Same here." I nodded. "It's too coordinated to be random, and why all at once? Mira, you want to help me with the portal?"

We moved into the weapons room next door to get my watch. Just as we lifted our wrists to channel our powers through the watches, Claire and Alex stepped through. Well, Claire carried Alex.

The right side of her chin was burned, as were her arms and hands.

"Damn dragons," Mira hissed.

I called for Jake to help Claire get Alex down to the healers.

"I'm okay." Alex's voice was a hoarse whisper. "They came out of nowhere. The portal was closed."

"I was around the corner helping with cleanup from the first raid, and I ran as fast as I could." Claire's normally sweet face was twisted in anger. "They were dead, but not before they hurt her."

Alex managed a weak smile. "They're lucky they were already dead. Our little sister was in quite a mood."

"Nobody messes with my family," Claire growled.

Jake and one of the other security agents came in to help carry Alex, but Claire wouldn't let go of her. We are all a bit protective of one another. We might give each other hell at times, but when it came down to it, we were as tight as any family could be.

"Claire, you have to put Alex down," Mira ordered, her voice firm but calm. "You know how tough it was to close our portals. Gillian's going to need our help, so let's get it done."

"What about me?" Alex's voice was hoarse, and edged with pain.

"You visit the healers and do what they say. We need you at full strength. God knows what's going to happen next," I told her.

Mira gave me a soft shove. "Don't say that, you'll jinx us all."

I rolled my eyes, and Alex gave a short chuckle. "Put me down, little sister." She patted Claire's hand.

Claire reluctantly handed over Alex. "I can stand," Alex grumbled as Jake took her in his arms.

"I'm sure you can," he told her, "right after we get you fixed up." He gave her a look that made me wonder if he had a bit of a crush on her. Jake was hot, in a stuffed-shirt kind of way.

Huh.

They left, and the three of us raised our wrists. Concentrating, I envisioned the portal and it hummed to life, but no matter what kind of power we shot through it, nothing happened.

"Holy crap. This is nuts." I pushed my hair back from my face. "Let's try again."

Nothing happened.

"What the hell?" I'd been a Guardian for a long time and there was no protocol for this. We'd always been able to shut down the damn things during emergencies.

"Maybe we should call Mom." From her tone, it was clear Claire wasn't happy with the idea. Bringing in our mother would mean we hadn't done our jobs properly. That, as I've mentioned before, was unacceptable to the matriarch of the Caruthers clan. I had no desire to be around when my sisters told her what had happened.

"You should definitely let her know what's going on, but I think I can solve our problem from the other side. I'm going to talk to King Arath."

"Do you think that's wise?" Mira frowned. "He'll know we've lost control and that's never good."

"Can you think of any other way?" I asked them both, and

they shrugged. "I'd rather deal with Arath than Mom. The portals to Maunra haven't been tainted with the black magic yet, and I have a feeling he'll know what to do."

They nodded.

I picked up my sword, and grabbed one of Bailey's guns just in case. I still had both of my knives in my boots from earlier. I twisted my shoulders and tried to relax. We'd all expended a great deal of power and I already felt the drain. It didn't help that breathing was difficult thanks to the broken ribs. *Suck it up, Gilly.*

"You guys see what you can do from this side. I'm going to have a short chat with the demon king." The blue light of the portal shot forth and I stepped through.

Thankfully I landed on my feet a few seconds later, but the jarring landing took my breath for a moment. I was met by a contingent of demons. This time there were ten different monsters. Some floated in circles around me; others stood at attention.

They weren't attacking, which was a good sign.

I pulled my translator out and stuck it in the right ear.

"We are the protective guard. Your life is in danger. King Arath wishes to see you now." The demon closest to me had a humanlike head. The rest of its body was covered in hair that fell to its feet.

I followed Cousin Itt to the castle door, the others circling us in protection.

Huh. I wonder what's going on here. Maybe Arath had experienced the same thing on Maunra as we had on Earth. This time the castle was filled to capacity. At first glance, every clan seemed to be represented. As we entered through the wooden doors, the crowd in the large hall parted and left us a clear path. Still, all those demons in one place made my skin crawl.

We went through an archway in the back of the room. I'd never been in this part of the castle. There was a long hallway with several doors. Cousin Itt knocked on a door.

Arath's gruff voice answered from the other side and I entered. The room held an enormous round table where thirty different demons sat. All of them looked my way. At least I think they did. Some of them had so many eyes it was difficult to tell.

I bowed my head toward the king. Even though I needed his attention immediately, I waited for him to speak, another sign of respect. It was important to uphold tradition when surrounded by so many of his subjects, and these guys were obviously either heads of clans or demons of power. Peasants didn't sit at the table with the king.

"Guardian, there is trouble in your world and mine. I am aware." The power emanated off of him in waves, his voice strong and so loud it made my eardrums hurt. The scary thing was I knew there was more power in him. He was only using a small percentage to control the others.

I couldn't keep my left eyebrow from rising, though I tried. "So you know about the portals?"

He nodded. "It's more serious than you can imagine. Your Earth portals are not the only ones affected. There are no barriers between worlds and chaos reigns."

Waving a hand around the table. "These are the heads of Maunra clans. They are here to discuss the thefts of several treasures. One clan believes another has stolen their precious items. Since this is so widespread, it is my belief that one group is responsible, or one being."

Interesting. Their treasures were stolen, too. The crowd around the table also explained why the castle was busting at the seams with creatures. No clan chief would travel without his guards. I stayed by the door, but moved just to the right. I didn't like the idea of having my back open to anything coming up behind me.

"We've been experiencing the same sort of thing, but they are targeting religious artifacts, most of it jewelry," I explained. "It isn't just your people. My sisters reported that Fae, dragons, and Nereids are involved. It's as widespread there as it is here."

Arath translated what I told him to the other clan members. They all seemed to settle down. It was one thing to think your neighbor stole your stuff, quite another to think someone from another world did. I had a feeling Arath wanted to prove to them that this was the case. That would make the clans work together, rather than fighting against one another. He really was a wise leader.

"I'm more than happy to investigate the situation, King Arath, but right now I have a pressing problem." I couldn't talk about not being able to close the portals in front of the demons. "When you have a moment I need to speak to you privately about the shift." It bothered me that I had to ask for help. My mother would be furious. Hopefully, Mira and Claire would be able to make her see reason.

Arath clapped his hands and Cousin Itt, who had led me to the room, appeared in the door again. "Take her to the Well Room. I will be there shortly."

I started to say something, but I stopped myself. It would be rude to respond once I'd been dismissed. I bowed my head again and followed the demon down the hall. Arath obviously had his hands full, but my problem needed an immediate solution.

The door at the end of the hall opened, and my guide stood beside it as I entered. I hadn't really known what to expect, but it wasn't what I saw before me.

Glass windows made up the outside wall, which looked out over an ocean view. As many times as I'd been to the castle, I'd never been privy to this. Most of my meetings took place in the main hall or in one of the side rooms off of it.

Day faded into night and a light snow fell from the purple clouds. The water looked like dark blue glass, almost as if it were frozen but not quite. It was beautiful. For the first time in twenty-four hours my shoulders relaxed. The tension headache I'd been feeling eased, and I took a deep breath. My ribs still ached, but not as badly as before.

Several small tables and chairs had been set up around the

room. I took the one in the center. It had the best view. As I continued to stare out onto the sea, my mind wandered. I didn't think about killing the demons who had jumped to my planet or the troubles with the portals. No, I thought about how great it would be to have a snowmobile and ride it along the snow-banks before me.

I leaned back in the carved wooden chair. Unlike most of the furniture in the castle, the ones here actually had com-fortable cushions. I wondered what my sisters were doing, and remembered that I needed to check with Georgia about the details concerning the Arts in Schools fund-raiser. Caruthers Corp. hosted the event, and Alex did most of the party plan-ning. I was in charge of getting donations, most of which had been taken care of months ago.

What the hell is wrong with me? I jumped up and ran for the door. It was locked from the outside. I chastised myself as I paced back and forth. *How could you be so stupid, Gillian?* I wanted to punch a wall, but I needed my strength.

When the door finally opened I was ready to kill the king. I drew my sword. He stopped short.

Brandishing it at him, I yelled, "What kind of magic are you using on me? You better stop it right now or I'll kill you."

CHAPTER

11

Moving into the Well Room, Arath belly-laughed. I held my sword at the ready.

"I mean it. Tell me what you did to me." I moved to the center of the room, my back to the ocean view.

He laughed again. "You have fire in your soul, and I do believe you might have tried to kill me. I sent you a relaxing, healing spell to help with your injuries."

As he pointed to my right shoulder I looked down. The shredded leather hung there, but the angry claw marks and clotted blood were gone.

I felt foolish, since I hadn't even noticed my own arm had healed. "I understand you wanted to help, but I'd appreciate you asking me beforehand. We have healers at home who take care of the Guardians."

Closing the door behind him, he moved toward me. "Showing up here with demon and human blood on your body was not a good idea." Now his voice was soft, almost seductive. "I can control my hunger, but there are those in the castle who cannot. It was not safe for you to stay in that room much longer, and that is why I healed your wounds."

My anger subsided. *Crap.* "You're doing it again."

"I assure you I am using no magic."

Oh, hell. His normal voice was like smooth whiskey and I really wanted a drink. I pinched the top of my nose. *Concentrate, Gillian.*

I opened my eyes to see Arath with a curious glint in his eyes. "Does your head pain you?"

"No. Look, I don't like asking for your help, but I have to get the portals closed immediately. Is there any way you can help me? I know your magic is strong, and hell, I friggin' hate this but could you please tell me if there is something we can do together?"

The demon king cocked his head as if he were contemplating an entirely different scenario.

The scary part was I liked the look in his eyes even though I should have been totally repulsed. *Jeez, get it together. You're tired. Just get this done and go home.* I turned away from the look that made my lower belly heat with fire and faced the ocean. "Please." I squeaked out the word.

"I did not explain to the clans because they would panic. The portal you opened to come here has already collapsed, tainted by the evil magic that pervades our universe. It is fortunate that it happened after you exited, or you would have been crushed."

He didn't sound happy about the idea, which was comforting in a way. "I believe we can combine our powers to solve several problems at once."

Something in his tone made me think he knew more than he said. "Did you do something? Is that why your people keep stealing things from Earth? I need to know."

His eyes flashed a fiery orange. "I am an honorable being. I only want peace. I do not use my power to harm. I have many riches and have no need to steal."

"My apologies, King Arath." I bowed my head. "I know that you are powerful. I can feel it rolling off of you."

"You have no idea what I can do." His hand thrust into the air. "I can close the portals here, but I can also help you to keep all the portals going to Earth, from every world, locked."

I coughed. "What?"

"Guardian, you waste my time and yours. We must do this quickly. I would do most anything to keep war from happening between worlds right now, as I am trying to establish peace on my planet. You came for help. I am giving you more than you ask. We must do this now. There is no more time." There was a sense of urgency in his voice.

Something in his tone made me stop. If he was worried, much like my mother, then things were bad.

You must shut everything down. He demanded this without speaking. I realized I could hear him in my mind. He took my hands in his and his touch sent a zinging sensation through my nerves. *Jeez.*

"Arath, I don't have enough power to shut them all at once and bind them. I have to do it one at a time." I tried to pull my hands away, but he held tight.

"You will use my power. Guide it as you need, but this must be done." I couldn't keep from staring at his face. His eyes glowed a deep fiery orange.

He wasn't telling me the truth—not all of it, anyway.

His frown deepened as if he knew why I hesitated. "Just do as I ask, and I will tell you what you need to know."

My lawyer instincts kicked in with the phrase "need to know." This time I yanked my hands from his. "I want the truth now!" I bit out the words and backed to the door, prepared to draw my weapons if necessary.

"I am King Arath, and you will make no demands, Guardian Key." He roared, using his lion's voice.

"You can growl all you want, Arath. You aren't using me unless I know why it's so important to you."

He paced back and forth. "I'm sworn to protect my people, and I cannot tell you."

"Then I can't help you." I tried to open the door but it was locked. "Open the door, Arath."

"I will not. You must see reason." He sighed. "This is best for both our worlds. Is that not enough? Why must you protest?"

Because I'm stubborn and I don't like being lied to. And something weird is going on here.

"Why can't you just tell me the truth and solve both our problems?"

He shook his head. "You are a fierce woman. I do not wish to battle with you."

My right eyebrow shot up. It does that when I'm amused. "Yeah, can't say I'm excited about fighting you to the death either." I had an icky feeling about how that might end. "So we need a compromise. You tell me why it's so important and I'll help you."

That made him laugh, but it wasn't a happy sound like before.

"Very well," he grumbled. "I will tell you this. There are those in my world who wish to do great harm to your people. You call it revenge. While I am not fond of the humans, I do not wish them dead. Hence, I shall close the portals."

"That's not really news. The demons have hated humans for centuries."

"Yes, but unfortunately for you, now they have the power to do something about it. Please, Guardian, trust me. We must do this quickly, before any more can cross over."

I had a feeling he still wasn't telling me everything, but technically it was my job to keep his kind out of my world.

"Fine. Do we do it here?"

He moved to the door. "Follow me."

We went back out into the hall and through the door to the left. The light was dim, but I could make out an ornate marble altar filled with candles. I noticed several piles of jewelry. Some looked like papal rings. There was artwork, and weapons. It looked like a large pile of gifts.

I cleared my throat.

Arath followed my line of sight. "I will explain later."

There was no use arguing with him. "Okay, now what?"

With a wave of his hand the door shut. "You must remove your weapons. The magic will make metal extremely hot."

A guardian never laid down her weapons, especially when visiting another world.

"You will come to no harm in my company." It really was as if he could read my mind. *That is a scary thought.*

I sighed as I took out my sword, knives, and gun and laid them on the counter behind me.

"Take my hands in yours." He reached out to me.

I did what he asked. The energy sizzled when we touched. His hands were rough, like they were used to hard labor. Not surprising, since before he was a king, he'd been a great warrior. Still his grip was gentle.

"You must close your eyes before we begin and keep them

so. The magic could blind you, if you open them. You must trust me."

I liked being able to see so I did what he said. Weird doesn't begin to explain how it felt holding hands with my eyes closed as if we were playing a game of some sort. Only this time the fate of many worlds depended on just how well we played.

"*Lak, nak to dol amp storn de ku.*" He repeated the phrase over and over again and the power built within us both. It began in my core, a deep warmth, and shot out through my hands.

I'd taken out my translator so it wouldn't burn my ear. I had no idea what the chant meant, but I could feel its power—his power. The louder his voice became the stronger the bond between us. I no longer knew where my hands ended and his began.

Even with my eyes closed I could see the bright light coming from his body. As tempted as I was to look, I remembered his warning. He hadn't exaggerated.

"You must concentrate, Guardian." Embarrassed that I'd been so easily distracted, I focused my mind on the glow I felt around me.

The energy pulled in every direction and suddenly I saw from Arath's eyes. They were focused on several dark swirling holes in a great expanse of the universe. As many times as I'd traveled through portals, I'd never actually seen one from space. The mass, which looked like several dark tornadoes, twirled so fast it made me feel unsteady to watch it.

"I am with you. Guide my power as you need." Arath's voice seemed to come from a great distance.

For a moment I didn't know what to do.

"Follow your instincts," he encouraged. "You have the power."

I took the golden glow I felt and mentally wrapped each of the portals I could see, then locked them with a large golden key I had imagined. I'd done this before with my sisters' help, but it was much easier this time around. In fact, rather than feeling tired after I closed the portals, my body became more energized with each one.

"Good." Arath's energy never wavered. If anything, he, too, grew stronger as each one slammed down.

As I locked the last one, I felt something dark and menacing reach out to me. This was the black magic the demon king had spoken of, and he hadn't overstated it. It was more powerful than anything I'd ever felt.

"No!" Arath's roar made me jump and my eyes opened for a split second. The shimmering gold light temporarily blinded me, and I squeezed them shut again, praying I hadn't just seared my retinas. For a moment it had looked as though my hands were holding the sun.

The demon king chanted again, never loosening his grip on my hands. The darkness I'd felt before dissipated. He let go of me, and I fell back against the counter where I'd left my weapons, my breath coming in gasps. The light was so bright I put my arm in front of my eyes to protect them. The energy surrounded me as if it might swallow me whole, then the room went dark.

Once I'd adjusted to the candlelight I watched as Arath moved toward the altar and knelt. He whispered as if repeating a prayer. A demon who prayed? The universe wasn't the only thing that had shifted. I felt like I'd just stepped into Surreal World.

As he rose and turned to me, I noticed he didn't seem tired at all. Quite the contrary. He seemed even stronger somehow. I'd never seen anything like it.

My hand slid behind me to my sword.

"What are you?"

CHAPTER

12

Before he could answer, pain seared through my head. "What the—" It was the last thing I said before I slid to the floor.

The next thing I knew, Arath held me in his strong, muscled arms.

I managed to open one eye. "What happened?"

"Your human form isn't made to channel the kind of energy you pulled from me. You had a temporary collapse, but you are fine now."

That reminded me of my earlier question, but this time we were interrupted by a pounding on the door.

"Yes," Arath bellowed.

"Master, the court awaits your arrival. The traitor has been brought to the center."

The crease in his brow told me Arath didn't look forward to whatever was about to happen.

"Traitor?"

"Yes. I must go." He sat me up on the counter. "I may be gone for a while, but I will return. Please do not leave this room. It is not safe for you to wander the castle."

His words were meant to be protective but they irked me more than anything.

"No disrespect, King Arath, but I can hold my own in a demon court and have done so many times in the past. I prefer not to hide away in a corner. It makes me look weak, and that's never a good thing for a Guardian."

It surprised me that he actually listened. "You must be careful. My people are anxious and they want a fight. It is difficult for them to understand what is happening with the shift. Many of them live by trading with other worlds, and now their means of travel have been closed off. You protect those portals, and they will see you as an enemy."

Pulling my shoulders back, I smiled. "It won't be the first time."

I followed behind Arath at a respectful distance until we arrived in the main hall. They had moved out his throne, a garish thing with a fur-lined seat. *PETA would have a field day with that one.* Funny how he seemed to make the monstrosity work. He'd turned his magic on full force and it was easy to see his people were enthralled. This king had something none of the others had—charisma and real power.

I didn't know exactly what he was, but it wasn't demon. Oh, that was part of his makeup, but Aunt Juliet's magic was clearly strong within him. He had melded our powers into one, and only an incredibly skillful mage could have done something like that.

Moving through the throng without touching anyone proved difficult. I didn't want to push my luck. I finally found a space where I could have my back to a wall and ready access to my weapons.

As he sat, his demon hordes knelt. I'd seen them bow before, but never had I seen them on their knees. At least what might have been knees. There were four-legged creatures, and flying ones, but they all showed a deep respect for the man.

The crowd stood and backed away. A nasty-looking monster with three dog-looking heads was shoved into the open area before Arath's throne.

"My lord." The demon behind the dog bowed. "I am Comdar and I have brought you the scum Santra. He is responsible for organizing the raids on the Earth planet."

The ugly dog howled. "It is a lie."

"Silence!" Arath bellowed at the creature. It cowered and made itself as small as possible. The king's power shot out in waves around the room. I could feel the tension.

"Santra, when you stole from my camp during the Loring War, what did I tell you?" The scowl on his face made Arath look very much like a demon. "Answer me."

The dog monster kept its heads down. "King Arath, I beseech you, please. I am a thief. I admit this. But I did not do this thing they say. I would not betray you, my lord."

"Your sniveling will not save your hide this time." The king walked down to the monster, which still had not looked up. He put his hand on the center head, and there was a hush in the crowd.

Arath's scowl never changed. "Santra, you are a liar. You did not plan this alone, but you were one of the conspirators."

The crowd grew excited. The anticipation of what might happen next had them salivating. They weren't so very different from humans in that respect.

The creature seemed to fold into itself in defeat.

"Clede, bring me my staff," Arath ordered his second in command.

The demon closest to him handed the king a long wooden pole with intricate carvings.

Arath seemed to grow taller, his chest wider, and his entire body turned red. Fangs shot out from his mouth and his eyes burned a bright orange. The staff became a stick of flames in his hand. "I sentence you to death, traitor." The fire engulfed the creature, and it became nothing more than a pile of ashes in less than five seconds.

Holy crap. Note to self: Do not get on Arath's bad side. Weird that he could go demon so quickly. I would have bet money that when he shared his power with me it was nothing but golden goodness. Now he looked very much like what I'd imagined the devil might when I was a child.

His actions seemed extreme, and yet I'd seen more than one demon lose its head in court. Nothing new there, but it bothered me that Arath had been the one to execute the traitor.

You think of him as a man. Never underestimate your opponent, Gilly. No matter what he seems to be, he's still a monster.

The crowd cheered. *Gruesome bunch.*

Arath banged the staff to the ground. "Those who betray the king—betray our world—die." The crowed hushed again. "Clede, remove the ashes and send them to his family as a reminder of what happens to traitors."

I'd met many a demon king, but never had I been afraid of one. Frustrated, angry, but never afraid. There was more to this guy than anyone might have imagined. In my early years as a Guardian I read every book on magical creatures available, and I'd never seen anything written about something like Arath.

The king returned to his natural state and sat on his throne. Several dignitaries drew his attention. I wanted answers but they would have to wait. Now that the portals were closed, my job here was done. I hadn't slept in two days and I needed to rest. That would be the easiest way to heal my body. Though I had to admit Arath's magic had done wonders. I could open and close my hand without pain, and my shoulder no longer ached. Even my ribs had healed.

Careful not to touch anyone, I slipped through the crowd. I was almost to the door when a female Colei stood in front of me. She had one horn shooting out of her forehead and she looked a bit like a mule standing on two legs. "The king has not dismissed the court. You may not leave." She crossed her sword against her chest.

I nodded. "Yes, I'm sure you're right, but I need to go. I mean no disrespect, your *king* knows this."

"You challenge me?" she screamed, and everyone in the crowd turned.

Yikes. Instinct had my hand on the sword at my back before she finished her sentence. "No, I do not challenge you. I need to go." Many pins could have been heard dropping in the silence that followed.

"Draw your weapon," she screeched. The crowd around us moved back.

Oh, great. I couldn't risk a glance back at Arath for fear of losing my head to the Colei's weapon. *Step in any time, Mr. King.* Then it dawned on me. He couldn't show favoritism to a Guardian. And if I thought about it I wouldn't want him to. I didn't want to kill the Colei, but I had no choice.

She stepped forward, her saber in one hand, claws growing out of the other. *Lovely.* I moved into fighting stance, holding the sword front and to the left. She was so fast I didn't even see her blade hit mine.

I ducked and threw out a kick to keep the weapon from slicing open my chest. I'd fought Colei on Earth, but their speed was much faster on their own planet. Of course, I was no slouch in the speed department.

I heard my mother's voice in the back of my head. "Don't think. Fight."

Jumping to the left, I crouched to miss another swing of her sword but the claws that came right behind it caught my neck and chest. She'd come dangerously close to hitting an artery.

The coppery smell of my own blood kicked my tired instincts into gear. I fought without thinking and moved as fast as the demon. I wasn't aware of the crowd or my surroundings, only of the will to survive. Only when she was on the ground, my sword in her chest, did I stop to think.

She was dead.

Another Colei demon jumped forward. This one was a male, and probably the mate of the other.

"Enough!" Arath roared. He stood near his throne. "She won the challenge."

The Colei hissed at me but didn't draw a weapon. He reached down and picked up the other demon and slung her over his shoulder. Those around him gave him a wide berth as he huffed out the castle door.

I wanted to say, "Um, you didn't ask the king's permission to leave," but it didn't seem appropriate.

Her claws had dug deep into my chest and blood poured from the leather. I needed one of our healers fast. I knew my body and it wouldn't be long before I passed out.

"King Arath, please forgive my haste in trying to depart. I

meant no harm or disrespect to you or your people, but I must go. I have business in my world."

An odd expression came over his face and he gave a strange smile. The devil was back.

"I'm afraid that's impossible, Guardian."

CHAPTER

13

As much as I wanted to, I couldn't fight the demon king in front of his subjects. "King Arath, may I request a private meeting? I promise I won't take much of your time."

He looked around the room in a way that said, "Forgive me, I must deal with the crazy demon slayer again."

"Certainly." Rising from his throne, he handed Clede the staff. The crowd parted to make room for him. I followed him down the corridor toward the door where I'd seen the ocean.

Using his hand to wave the door shut, he then motioned me to a table. "I will explain while I heal your wounds."

I acquiesced only because my energy was flowing out of my body by the second. Leaning back in the chair, I glanced down at my chest. There was little skin left just above my left breast, the bones exposed.

"Close your eyes," Arath whispered.

I did what he asked, and tried to relax. Once again I could see the golden glow through my lids. My chest burned, and at one point if felt as if my heart might explode.

"Take a deep breath," he whispered.

I did and inhaled a calming eucalyptus mist that made my shoulders drop and pulled the fire from my chest. I wanted to see how he'd done this, but the glow was still bright and I didn't want to risk blindness.

"You shut and locked all of the portals with our magic." Arath pulled his hand from my chest and moved to my right thigh, which had seen the wrong edge of the Colei's blade. "If we open one for you to travel home, we risk disrupting the spell and opening them again. The spell will grow in strength as time passes and will protect the portals from the darkness, but as I said, it will take time and you must stay on Maunra."

Panic rose inside of me. I couldn't be stuck on Maunra. I had to tell my family about the dark magic, and goodness only knew what had jumped through those portals before we closed them. Earth might be experiencing a plague of demons. I also wanted to talk to my mother about Arath. I didn't know what he might be, but I was more curious than ever to find out.

I'd just seen him reduce a demon to a pile of ash, and he'd healed me almost as good as new, even though I'd been near death. At the very least near passing out.

"You will come to no harm here," Arath's voice soothed. "When it is safe, I can take you home through a portal by adding my magic for protection, but it will be twenty-four of Earth's hours before I can do this. That's when the magic will be at its strongest."

I shook my head. "We are in the middle of a battle on Earth. I can't leave my family wondering what has happened to me."

"I can send a message, that you are safe and will return soon." He moved his hand from my thigh. "This is how it must be done. There is no other way."

I chewed on my lip.

"I told you before that your planet was not the only one under siege. There are rumors of war here on Maunra."

Before I could say there were always wars on Maunra, he held up a hand.

"We are in a time of peace. You see how the clans respond. Many have agreed to disagree, because they understand that we must band together to fight this new foe. The same enemy who wishes to destroy your planet."

I leaned to the side and put my arm on the table. "Do you have any idea who is doing this?"

"No, but it is more than one person. We've had several robberies, as have you, and they all take place at the same time. This tells me it is a group, one that has dark magic at its disposal."

"But the demons I killed were from here, and you said that

the dog thing had conspired to set up the raids. You executed him for it."

Arath leaned back and crossed his arms against his chest. "I gave him peace because his mind was no longer his own. An outside force controlled him. One that was able to manipulate him. The darkness you saw as we closed the portals is seeping into all of our worlds. I know we have more traitors here, as I am certain there are human traitors on Earth. It is only through them we will be able to trace the darkness. It fills them, controls them. My guess is the same thing is happening not just here, but throughout the universe."

I made a motorboat sound with my lips. Being a Guardian meant always being ready for the weirdness to happen, but this was beyond anything I'd come across before. Fighting a bad guy we couldn't see would be no easy task.

My mother and Aunt Juliet had been with the council for weeks now, which meant they were well aware of what was going on. When she had mentioned that things were going downhill fast, I believed her, but I didn't realize at the time just how serious the threat had become.

"So, what do I do for the next twenty-four hours?"

Arath stood. "I have arranged quarters for you so that you may rest."

I wondered when he'd done this, but with Arath, obviously surprises were the name of the game. A short nap didn't sound like a bad idea. I didn't need as much sleep as most people but I'd been going all out for more than forty-eight hours. I'd fought battles here and on Earth, and I honestly needed a little downtime.

We didn't go back out into the hall, but through a side door and up three flights of stairs. I saw several sets of double doors.

The nearest doors swung open before we even reached them, and I knew Arath had something to do with that. As we entered, I caught my breath. It was different from anything I'd seen in the castle. It looked like a hotel suite at the W, with modern furnishings. Everything was in a combination of creams, browns, and soft blues.

"It's beautiful."

He nodded as I followed him in. "I saw a room similar at a resting house on Chndre. It was done by Fae who were known for their artistic ability, and I had it re-created here." He pointed toward a doorway. "There is a bathing room through there, and leathers that are close to your size in the chest at the end of your bed. This will be a restful place for you?"

"Yes. Thank you."

He turned toward me and put a hand on my shoulder. "You fought well today, Guardian."

I didn't know what to say. "Thanks."

As he walked back to the door he gave me final instructions. "There are locks on this door controlled by my magic, once you slip in this key." He handed me a small key that looked as if it were made of diamonds. "No one will be able to enter. I give you my word."

The doors shut behind him and I put the key in. A series of unseen bolts slid into place. The demon king had given his word, but I kept my sword within reach the entire time I readied for bed, and as I fell asleep, my hand slipped to the handle.

I woke eight hours later feeling as though I'd slept for days. *That was one long nap.* My body hummed with energy, and hunger gnawed at my stomach. I found the "leathers" Arath had mentioned. There was a soft, loose-fitting blouse with a drawstring at the neck, a leather vest, and a pair of leather pants I might have found at a cute boutique in SoHo.

I slipped the key from the door and the locks opened.

There at the doorstep was a sandwich and tea set. There was no one in the hallway. I picked up the tray and put the key back in the lock. Sitting cross-legged on the bed, I pulled the pieces of bread apart and discovered peanut butter and honey. It was exactly what I wanted. I took two bites and it tasted just like it would have at home. *Peanut butter on Maunra; the universe really is whack.*

I poured the tea into the cup and wafts of cinnamon and vanilla goodness steamed toward me. I appreciated the fact that Arath had gone to great pains to make me feel at home.

I thought about all that had transpired the last few days and I missed my sisters and Bailey. I was so used to running troubles past them and making them my sounding board. This universal shift, whatever it was, would affect us all. From the way we'd been kept busy, that was more than obvious.

The Caruthers sisters could handle it, no matter what. We'd been groomed for this our entire lives: to protect our world from others who would do it harm. It seemed funny that I might soon long for the days of catching and killing the occasional jumper.

A knock on the door tore me away from my thoughts.

"Yes," I said as I moved to the door.

"It is me," Arath announced from the other side.

I slid the key out.

"You are refreshed?" He was dressed in his jeans again, and this time wore a long white shirt made the way mine was. The smell of cloves was strong on him, and I wondered if that was his natural scent.

I hated that I was so drawn to him. "Yes." I tried my best to pretend my traitorous body wasn't hot for him.

"You have something here." His thumb caressed the top of my lip, sending warm sensations down to parts of my body that heated instantly. As he licked the small bit of peanut butter from his thumb, my heart beat faster. "This is good."

I backed away and turned toward the bed. My heart raced and I took a calming breath. "I'm curious how you happen to have peanut butter on hand, and where do you find Levi's?" *Especially ones that hug your incredible butt like they do.*

"The markets here have many things from other worlds." He moved closer to me. "My favorite Earth food is honey. As a treat my father would give it to my brother and me. The color reminds me of your hair." His voice was whisper soft.

"Are you flirting with me?" I couldn't keep from smiling as I turned to face him.

He shrugged. Touching my shoulder, he drew me closer. "You have a power that pulls me to you, and I find it difficult to stay angry even when I know I should. I thought of you in here. I wanted to watch you sleep."

My body reacted to his words as if he'd been stroking me. I did my best to change the subject. "So, how is it going out there?" I waved a hand toward the door. "Any news on what's happening with the darkside?"

He moved to within two inches of me and I felt drawn to him. "The council is aware of the problem and is working toward a solution."

I smiled. "That's politicospeak for they don't know what the hell is happening."

He gave me a faint smile and his face leaned closer to mine as if he were examining me. "I fear you are right, Gillian." And then he kissed me. He wasn't tentative with that initial contact. His lips pressed hard and invaded my mouth in such a sensual way, I lost all thought of anything else. A hand caressed my back and my arms curled around his neck. When he finally lifted his head from mine, my body felt like a puddle of melted butter.

"Wow. That was—"

"Interesting." His eyebrow went up.

"Yes." I wondered if he felt as wobbly as I did. Probably wasn't possible since his body looked as though it were made out of carved stone. There wasn't a soft spot on him. I knew this because of the hardness pressing against my thigh. Rather long and large.

I cleared my throat and stepped to the right, pretending to look out the window. But the snow-covered mountains were nothing but a blur. The demon king had just kissed me, and darned if I hadn't kissed him back.

Can't say that's ever happened before.

"There is something I would like to show you."

I had a choice of saying something incredibly lewd, but held my tongue. "Sure. I've nothing but time right now."

"You will need your outerwear; we must travel through the snow for a short time."

I opened the wardrobe and pulled out my leather jacket. I'd done my best to clean it before I went to bed. I couldn't imagine what he wanted to show me, but I had a feeling blindly following Arath could lead to untold adventures.

CHAPTER

14

He took me through a side door and outside to the stables. I wasn't sure what to expect, but the large birds were a complete surprise. They had the body and neck of an ostrich, but their heads looked like dragons.

"What are these?"

"Lumdups. They are a breed of wild dragon crossed with our Dupnons. In battle they are used to fly short distances, and they run very fast." I'd seen a Dupnon before. It looked like something between a buffalo and a horse. It was a strange-looking creature, but then most things on Maunra were. Well, except for Arath.

He held out his hand, and one of the creatures bowed and then came a little closer for a rub on the head.

"It seems everything in your world bows to its king." I moved a little closer, more out of curiosity than anything. The creature's head and neck looked as though they had been made out of mother-of-pearl, the feathers soft and fluffy on its back and sides. The legs were much thicker than those of an ostrich, but shaped the same way, with deadly looking claws.

Arath took my hand. "I will help you climb on."

I stiffened. "What?"

"We will use the animals to travel so that I may show you the surprise."

I'm not a small girl, but he easily lifted me and put me on the back of the dragon bird. "I—I'm not really comfortable with this. There's no saddle. How do I hold on?" As I said it, two small wings came out of the creature's lower neck.

"Hold on here." Arath pointed to the wings. "You need not worry, you will balance once we are in the air."

What! In the air? Great, Gillian, just great. What are you going to do now? Tell him that you can travel twice the speed of light but you're afraid of flying on a giant bird thing? Guardians show no fear. I sighed.

He climbed on another one and suddenly we were airborne. I didn't know if I was supposed to guide it, but the thing seemed to know where it needed to go. Before I had time to even think about screaming we landed on the other side of the forest in the middle of a small village.

Arath helped me climb down and then motioned for me to follow him into a building. The structure was made out of the same gray stone as the castle, and looked chilly and barren from the outside.

The inside was quite a different story. We entered a room with several rows of tables. Tiny demon children of all different breeds sat with paper and paints. When they saw Arath, they stood and bowed.

He waved his hand for them to sit down and continue. As he walked among them he made kind comments about their work, even though the actual subject of the art was sometimes difficult to determine.

"This is wonderful. I had no idea your schools were interested in the arts."

"Education in all things is important if one is to be a wise warrior." Arath patted another child on the head. "The art is new to our world. But our children are learning quickly." He held up a rough picture of what looked like a lake and mountains. "Very good."

I smiled. "Yes, it is. Did you know about my passion for the arts? Especially trying to get the arts back into public schools in America?"

He nodded. "I know many things about you, Guardian. We have always had our music and some crafts, but the painting is new. It will add color to our world, so that we may match the beauty that surrounds us in nature."

I'd seen the purple sunsets, and pristine wilderness, so I wasn't so sure they'd be able to match it, but it made me admire Arath all the more.

"You are surprised." He watched me with those glowing eyes of his.

"Yes, very. This really is wonderful. Art is a way children can express themselves, when perhaps words won't come. It allows them to open their imagination and to dream." I happened to look down at a catlike demon. I couldn't tell if it was a girl, but it looked like one. Think jaguar but with a human face and searing green eyes. She was beautiful, but that wasn't what caught my attention. She'd drawn a perfect portrait of Arath. She even had the color of his eyes perfectly tinted. "King Arath?"

My speaking scared the child and she ducked under the table. I bent down so I could see her. "It's okay." I smiled, but she scooted farther away from me. I looked up to see the other children eyeing me warily.

"I'm sorry. Can you speak to her and tell her that I only wanted to say how beautiful her picture is?"

Arath made a soft mewling sound, and whispered words into the air. I didn't have my translator in my ear so I had no idea what he said, but the child popped her head out over the bench and smiled with her large pointed teeth.

Her king picked up the picture and made a big fuss over it, and in that moment something crazy clicked in my heart. A demon ruler who had a hot bod and a good soul, or at least who did in the right circumstances. It was almost too much for this Guardian to take.

He nodded his head toward her. "She is giving the art as a gift, and I told her it will have an honored place in my home."

The place could use a little color. Other than the battle-ridden tapestries and sconces, there wasn't much to brighten up the place.

I remembered the art I'd seen in the altar room, but this wasn't the time or place to ask about it.

Clede entered the building on a cold burst of air. He didn't have to say anything. Arath knew he was needed.

After carefully rolling the picture and putting it in the pack on his back, he waved good-bye to the children.

When we made it outside I could see he was agitated.

"What's wrong?"

He grumbled. "There is trouble at the castle and we must go immediately."

I wanted to question him further but he plopped me down onto the Lumdup. Before I could even my open my mouth we were in the air and then on the ground again.

"Clede will take you to your rooms, and a meal will be sent up." He rushed off without a backward glance.

The grumpy demon pointed toward the castle. I followed him through the snow and upstairs to the warmth of my room. "I don't suppose you could tell me what's going on?"

He stared at me for one creepy moment and then slammed the door.

Great. Just great.

CHAPTER

15

I do not like being a prisoner under any circumstances, and I certainly didn't approve of being locked in a room at the castle. My anger at Arath boiled out of control.

"How dare he do this," I said to the bed linens. "I've proven myself to him more than once. I can certainly handle his demon hordes. None of the other kings thought it necessary to hide me away."

I slammed a fist into the mattress. "First he kisses me and shows his outreach work so that I'm so gooey for him, it's sick. Then he locks me away. Ack. What am I doing here?"

Soft. That's what had happened. I'd gone soft. After crappy Emilio I'd been so desperate for a man to show interest that I'd thrown myself at the demon king. Ick. I thought back among

the previous monarchs of Maunra. They were hideous creatures I didn't even want to be in the same room with, and now
I'd been macking on one of them.

"He might look human, but he isn't." I thought back to my
conversation with my mother. "Well, maybe he's part human. But
I saw him go all fiery red, so there's definitely demon in there."

What kind of creature had the power to see portals from
space and close them with magic so strong I'd never seen anything like it? I'd read ancient texts about magical beings so
powerful they could draw energy from around them to move
through space and time. It wasn't anything anyone in recent
history had done. If anything, that proved Arath was far from
human.

You kissed him, and you liked it.

Disgusted with myself, I wanted to slam the tattoos on my
wrists together and go home, but I knew it wasn't the smart-
est choice. I'd probably end up floating somewhere in darkness
seconds before I died from lack of oxygen.

Right now, Earth was safe from the demon hordes. Arath
may have been right about the dark magic seeping into the
portals if we tampered with the lock; so opening one was definitely out of the question.

I growled in frustration. "The demon king isn't the only
one who can roar."

I tried the door but it wouldn't budge. Taking the diamond
key from my pocket, I slid it into the lock. Nothing happened.
I turned it but it wouldn't budge.

My fists tightened and the nails dug into my hand.

I sat down on the edge of the bed, and thought about the many ways the demon king could accidentally die.

"There is trouble." Arath slammed his way into my room.

"You're right about that. Do you know about the laws against taking a Guardian prisoner?" I held my sword at the ready.

He stepped back, eyeing the point of my sword with a look that had nothing to do with fear and everything to do with amusement. That he didn't deem me a threat was the last straw.

I adjusted my stance.

"Do not be foolish, Guardian. I did not keep you prisoner. I only protected you. There had been an ambush at the castle while I was away and I did not know what to expect when we returned." He didn't move but he had a cocky look on his face that made me want to punch him.

"That may be, but I'm perfectly capable of holding my own in any attack. I've been trained for—"

"The magic grows strong again," he interrupted. "The beings that attacked the castle were not under their own control. If they'd killed me then the portals would have opened, and I feel certain this was their purpose. The portals are holding, but if I'm to get you home we must do it quickly."

At the mention of home, my body lost the tension it held. "I thought we had to wait."

"If the dark magic continues, we won't be able to use the portals without fear of them collapsing. Your human body would disintegrate within a few seconds if we tried."

Jeez. I'm going to start calling him Mr. Happy News. "Okay, so on to plan B. What do we do?" I slid my sword into its harness and the knives into my boots. The guns went in the holsters.

"Vex."

My head snapped up. "You shouldn't have access to a Vex portal from Maunra. We destroyed all of them." Vex was a dangerous mode of transport. The portals used the power of black holes. Sometimes you made it to your destination; other times you ended up in a never-ending sea of blackness just before you died from the crushing force of the hole.

"There is one left, to be used at the king's discretion. It is in our treaty. Every planet is allowed one for emergency situations."

I paced back and forth. "The chances of me making it home are slim, you have to know that."

"You are wrong. With your power and mine, I can guide you there."

It was risky, but I'd seen what Arath could do. Maybe he could handle a Vex tunnel. "And this is the only way?"

He nodded again.

"Fine, let's go." I had to die someday, and anything was better than sitting in this room one more second.

"There is one thing." He motioned me to follow him. "Have you ever been in one of the tunnels?"

We moved down several steps. "No," I said to his back. "We are trained to avoid certain death if possible."

"You joke, but the reason your kind often get lost is the energy from the holes. They create realities, unkind ones. You call them nightmares come to life. You must be prepared for what you might see, and you must know it is not real. No matter what you see or hear, concentrate on my voice."

Again with the comforting news. Jeez. "Will you be coming with me?" We'd made it to the castle entry without seeing anyone. The bodies of those who had lost the battle were gone. I was glad. Demons don't smell very good as a whole, and they were particularly rancid when they were dead.

"Not physically, but I will be with you just the same. You will hear my voice until you reach the other side. Remember, the things you see are not real. This is important."

"I understand." We now stood in the middle of the great hall.

He faced me and took my hands. "Remember what we did in the altar room? This will work in much the same way. I will connect with the door to the Vex." He turned me so that my back was to him. "When I let go of you, move forward, keeping your eyes closed for as long as possible. Concentrate on my voice."

I took a deep breath. I would never say it out loud, but I was scared to death. If he lost control—

"I will not fail you, Gillian." His lips were so close to my ear it felt like a kiss. He'd used my name. Hands sliding to my neck, his body pressed against the back of mine. Hard muscles and strength, it took all my wits to keep from leaning into him.

"Close your eyes, and move forward." I did and I felt his warmth wrap around me. I was no longer frightened. I'd been surrounded by a warm glow of comfort. I took a few steps and suddenly my body was weightless in the air. I kept my eyes closed, but I heard strange noises, and it was difficult not to look.

"Listen to my voice, Gillian. A few minutes and you will be home."

A child yelled and reflex made me glance ahead. A man held two children by the scruffs of their necks. He shook them as if wanting to break their bones by the force of it. They didn't cry, but both had fierce expressions on their tiny faces.

For some reason I knew it was Arath and his brother and I wondered if their father had been cruel. I wanted to reach out to the children and take them with me. In fact, I wanted to do that more than anything.

"Do not hesitate," Arath's voice chided. "Move forward; you see only what the energy wants you to see."

I closed my eyes and this time it was a woman's scream that made them open. I saw Markie, her chest bleeding. "Gillian, help me, please." Tears streamed down her cheeks and I couldn't keep from calling out to her.

"Markie. I'm so sorry." My arms reached out of their own volition. I started to move toward her. The blood poured from her chest and I knew I had to stanch the flow if she were to survive.

"No!" Arath's voice bellowed. "Your friend is already dead. You cannot help her. These are tricks. Keep moving forward, Gillian. Whatever you see it is not real. Send your mind forward. You are almost there."

The demon king was right. Markie died days ago. These were illusions. It was difficult but I shut my eyes again. The screaming stopped.

A pain shot through my back as a force pushed me through something. I felt cold steel and pushed against it. The force shoved me through into the control room. I was home. *Thank you, Arath.* I knew that last bit of force came from him.

I turned sideways to keep from hitting the wall across the room head-on and crashed into it with my shoulder.

"You always do know how to make an entrance, Gilly." Bailey shot a hand down toward me. "Come on, we've got work to do."

CHAPTER

16

"Where the hell have you been? Mom was about to call for reinforcements." Bailey tried to drag me out of the control room.

"Hold on, little bro, I've got to unload my weapons."

He looked down to see I held the new guns he had developed.

"Oh, fun. Did you get to use them on the demon hordes? And what the hell kind of portal was that you came through? I thought it was going to suck the house through it, it's so strong."

"No to the guns. Sorry. The way things are going, I'm sure I'll get to use them soon. As for the portal"—I put my sword and harness back on the wall—"it was a Vex."

His head snapped back so fast he looked like Linda Blair in *The Exorcist*. I hated that movie.

"Mom's going to be royally pissed." He shook his head. "I don't think I want to be in the room when she finds out."

I shoved him out the door and into the hallway. "Thank you for your support, but it happened to be the only way I could get home. There's some nasty black magic causing havoc in the universe."

He held up a hand. "I know. That's why I'm supposed to take you straight to the conference meeting. Ginjin is here from Xerxes. They were attacked and from the sound of things it was bloody as hell. Alex and Mom are in there getting the details. They said for you to come in immediately and report about what's happening on Maunra."

I sighed. Ginjin was a dragon warrior whose army had never lost a battle. If there was a problem on his planet, all hell really had broken out. I also wasn't looking forward to being in the same room with Ginjin and Alex. The tension alone would be suffocating. After the last three days I needed a break.

"Do they really need me? I can send them both e-mails. I have a ton of work to do at the office."

He snorted. "Sure. Why don't you just stop in and tell Mom you're defying a direct order?" Bailey turned to smirk and almost tripped on the carpet.

"Ha. Karma got you." I smirked right back. "Fine, take me to the war room, but I swear if he starts breathing fire like the last time we tried to have a meeting with him, I'm liable to kill him."

Bailey had the nerve to snicker. "Remember what happened to your eyebrows?" He couldn't see me glare at his back, but I'm sure he felt it.

"Who else is in there?"

"Jake, Marcel from the council, and some guy named Nabobi. I'm not really sure who or what he is. He looks human, but my spidey sense says nope to that. He and Marcel seem to be pretty tight."

Marcel was one of the more persuasive council members and a good friend of my mother's. I was certain that was why he'd been called in. He also had a way of calming down the room when things were heated. I had a feeling his services would most definitely be needed with Alex and Ginjin sharing space.

Dead silence. That was what met me when I walked into the room. My mother glared, and everyone's attention turned to me as I entered.

"Nice of you to join us, Gillian," Mother bit out. Notice I say "Mother." It's hard for me to call her "Mom" when she's in full bitch mode, and she was definitely that.

"There were problems on Maunra when we shut down the portals. The black magic that is seeping in is strong there," I said quickly. "I was able to shut down all of their portals, but then it created a problem for me returning. I ended up having to come through a Vex tunnel."

Mom's angry stare became a frown. There was concern there.

"You know you aren't supposed to travel through the Vex tunnels. You could have been killed." Alex stood and hugged me. "My God, Gilly, what were you thinking?" The ends of her long black ponytail had been singed and she smelled of smoke. Whatever had been going on, she'd been in the middle of it. I checked her over to see if she had any wounds.

At first glance she seemed okay, but I never knew with Alex. She was good at hiding her pain. I shrugged. "That I had to get home, because I'm not supposed to be protecting Maunra. That's King Arath's problem. It was his idea for me to travel through the Vex." I didn't mention that if it hadn't been for him, I wasn't sure I would have made it.

Mom's fist came down on the table. "We will discuss this later. Gillian, take a seat next to your sister. You mentioned they had problems there. Perhaps you'd care to elaborate."

I looked around the table to once again find all eyes on me. Nabobi, who was the only one I hadn't met before, had an intense look. He was humanlike, but his body looked as though he'd spent some time on the rack. He was reed thin and pale, with one blue eye and one yellow one. Other than that, he looked like anyone else you might see on the street.

Marcel was a Loundan. His world, Sclocner, had been one of the few places where beings from several species had lived in harmony. But rebel forces from another dimension blew the planet to bits with a powerful weapon before anyone even knew the bad guys had arrived. Marcel and a few others survived because they had been visiting other planets.

I cleared my throat. "The black magic encircled all of the portals and King Arath says that several of his subjects are being controlled by whatever it is. There was a battle just before I left between Arath's forces and demons who tried to take over the castle. Ar—the king says that the demons were controlled by whatever this magic is. The same thing happened with the demons who came here to steal the treasures. They were controlled by something from the outside."

Marcel clasped his hands together in prayer position. He happened to be slightly furry, with his whole lycanthrope thing happening, but he had always been kind and thoughtful. He looked a bit like a human bear with long robes. "This is disturbing, and Ginjin has given the same kind of report. His own soldiers turned against him."

I'd been avoiding looking at the dragon warrior, but I glanced his way. A large gash went from the top of his forehead to just above his right eye, and his shoulder looked injured. His long silver hair was matted with blood.

While he looked human now, when his wings came out of his back his face transformed into that of a dragon, though he could breathe fire in any form. "Are you okay?" I couldn't help but ask. He looked pretty darn mangled.

Alex shot me a glare.

"I don't mean any disrespect," I added. "I only wanted to know if you were—I'm sorry. It's none of my business."

Ginjin stared at me for a moment. "I am alive, Guardian, but I am worried for the welfare of my people. I should be there instead of here babbling about things that do not concern me." He glared at Marcel and Mom.

I saw Alex make a slight movement with her hand, as if she were touching his knee to calm him down. He glanced over at her and nodded.

Hmmm. I'm definitely going to have to ask her about that.

"What is happening concerns the entire universe, Ginjin." My mother's tone was firm and to the point. "From what Gillian tells us, the magic is incredibly strong in Maunra, too. We have our mages on your planet now, and our forces are working furiously to establish peace. When you return you will see this."

The dragon warrior stood. "Talking solves nothing. We need action. I understand the council's position and I know you want to help, but if we don't work quickly my planet will no longer exist. My people will kill each other." In that moment the fierce dragon warrior look defeated, and his voice grew hoarse.

Alex had nothing but concern in her eyes.

Yes, I most definitely have to ask her about that.

"We have our plan in place," my mother said. "We will focus on Xerxes for now. The only other world in immediate danger is Maunra and it sounds to me as if King Arath has that under control." She stood. "Gillian, I'd like you to keep in contact with Arath. We are opening a new portal tomorrow, which is being designed by the mages to be protected from the dark magic. Alex, you and I will follow Ginjin home to see what we can do there. Marcel, if you will, please advise the council about what we have learned concerning Arath's planet. He may have already sent a report, but since communication is difficult, let's make sure."

Marcel nodded. Nabobi followed him out.

"Hey, Gilly, I need to talk to you." Alex stepped toward me. "You missed your fitting in Milan for your dress for the ball. I had a few shipped here, so you'll need to decide which one to wear and have it fitted. Cherise said for you to call her when you get back."

Only Alex could talk about saving the world one minute and fashion the next—with equal importance.

I tried to interrupt to ask about the dragon warrior, but she held up a hand. "I know you have questions, but I don't have time right now. Everything is set for the party. Georgia has everyone's numbers and there shouldn't be any troubles. I confirmed the guest list last night. The caterer will be working on-site, as will the designers. I called Colin in for some last-minute help. He'll make sure it all goes off without a hitch. I'm going to try and make it back, at least for a little bit. We need to make appearances whenever possible."

I nodded. "Thank you. I'm sorry I couldn't get back to help you out."

She hugged me. "I'm just glad you're safe, and stay away from those damn Vex tunnels. I'll tell you more about"—her voice became hushed—"Ginjin later. All you really need to know is he's pissed because I saved his life."

I laughed. "You're always so damn inconsiderate."

She smiled. "Tell Mira and Claire that I've also had their dresses sent here. And I bought Bailey a new tux. The man has at least twenty of them and he still shows up crumpled. Maybe we should just hire him a full-time valet."

"Personal assistant and stylist," I added.

"Takes a village to raise a Bailey." She snorted and we both giggled.

"Alexandra." Mom's sharp voice pierced our fun.

She rolled her eyes: "Gotta run."

I waved good-bye and then went to see what she'd put together for my party wardrobe. It sounded crazy, considering the state of the universe, but I was kind of excited to see the dresses Alex had picked out for me. A little frivolity would do me good. Trying on evening gowns and designer shoes was exactly what I needed.

CHAPTER

17

After a quick shower I called Mira and Claire. Like I said before, the best thing about being a Guardian was traveling across the universe in a matter of seconds. Mira had been at a medical conference in New York, Claire in Fiji scouting locations for her new documentary. A few minutes later we were gathered in my room with our dresses hanging in every doorway.

"My God, she really did go overboard this time," Mira laughed.

Between the three of us a good portion of the hottest designers were represented. Alex was so good about knowing exactly what looked best on our bodies. I knew from a quick glance at the hangers that all three dresses would be amazing on me. The hardest part would be picking a color.

"I know it's lazy, but I may have Charise and her team tailor all three so I don't have to make a decision today." I pulled my hair into a ponytail. "You know me, I sort of go with my mood and lately I never know what state of mind I'm going to be in."

"I hear ya," Claire said as she stepped into a pink Carmen Marc Valvo number. "Lately, I have so many wounds, I never know what I'm going to need to cover up." With her hair, the soft pink dress looked incredible on her. She scrunched up her nose. "I don't know about pink. I'm trying to look mature so the Hollywood crowd takes me more seriously."

I snorted. "Hey, baby, with that crowd youth is everything. I think you should play it up big time. Be the wunderkind that you are."

Mira slipped on a coffee-colored dress that was nothing less than stunning. "Holy cow. Who made that one? You wouldn't even have to have it altered."

"It's Zac Posen. I swear he designs with my body in mind."

Probably didn't hurt that she had the body of a goddess. While we were all relatively thin, Mira had curves in all the right places.

"So are you going to tell us what happened on Maunra? Bailey said you were in on the council meeting, too."

"Oh, yeah, life's been a laugh a minute the last few days." I took a deep breath and then relayed the most important bits, including that Alex and Ginjin seemed to have found a tentative truce.

"You can't be serious. They hate each other," Claire said as she pulled on a short little black and white polka-dot dress with a deep red sash around the waist.

"I know. She said she'd explain later but it had something to do with saving his life. Though I have to admit, he didn't seem very grateful."

Mira put on a flowing sea green gown that was cut so low on her back that she wouldn't be bending over during the evening's events. She turned to look at herself in the mirror. "Oh, this is a disaster waiting to happen. You know what a klutz I can be. One wrong move and I'm mooning the glitterati."

I belly-laughed for the first time in ages, so hard I could barely catch my breath. "God, I needed this. Things have been so intense the last week or so."

Claire nodded. "It's only going to get worse. I say we enjoy life while we can." She winked.

"Oh, my God, you are so in love." Mira wagged a finger at her.

Claire giggled.

Mira slid off the last dress and threw on her T-shirt and jeans. "Spill it, Tiny." At five four, Claire's always been the shortest in the bunch. With her long blonde hair, she really does look like a miniature surfer girl.

"It's too new. I don't want to jinx anything." Claire slid on her shorts and blouse.

"Since when do you not spill a secret?" Mira chided.

"Fine. It's my new cameraman. The guy the Save the Tiger Sharks charity sent out to help me with the documentary. It's nothing yet; we just had kind of a moment today." She glanced at her watch. "I'm hoping we have a longer moment very soon. I'm supposed to meet him for breakfast in an hour at this little place on the beach." She held up the dresses. "I can't decide which one I like better. I'm sort of leaning toward the pink, but it seems a weird color to wear in November."

For chicks who save the world, it was kind of funny that we couldn't make up our mind about a couple of dresses.

"I'll see you guys later. I've got to pop back for my little date." She winked as she walked out the door.

Mira left not long after, and I decided to check in with Kyle.

"I don't have anything yet," he said. "I'm in New York following up on a lead. Jake said you guys were having some bigtime otherworldly trouble."

The universe has gone to hell, but other than that everything is great. "Nothing we can't handle. Did you find some kind of connection between Markie and Emilio?"

"No. I still don't know where that rumor came from. I asked the reporter point-blank, and I got the 'I never reveal my sources' crap."

"It's ludicrous. We run in the same circles, so if someone had seen them together they would have called."

"True. Your crowd loves the gossip. Listen, I'm here at my meet. I'll let you know what I find out."

After hanging up I was anxious. I felt like calling Emilio and asking him if he had also been screwing one of my best friends, but I couldn't bring myself to do it.

I ran down to the gym and put on some gloves. An hour later I felt much better, though our latest punching bag had seen better days. That was my fourth one this month. One of the disadvantages of being superstrong was I wore out a lot of exercise equipment. I had to stop running on treadmills because even on the fastest speed they couldn't keep up and I burned out the motors.

After another shower, I decided to sleep for a couple of hours before catching up on work. It wasn't long before I found myself in the middle of another dream. No murders in this one. My toes curled in the warm sand as I watched the waves roll in. The sun lowered and dipped down into the horizon, giving everything a soft glow.

My back tingled and I knew someone stood behind me. I turned to see Arath there. All he wore were those button-fly jeans. His bronzed muscles rippled as he walked, and I had a hard time swallowing.

"You shouldn't be here," I finally managed.

Giving me a wicked smile, he reached out and took my hand. "It's your dream, Gillian."

"True." I loved the way he said my name with that British accent. "Still. I don't think it's appropriate."

"You may have noticed I don't care much for rules," he whispered as he pulled me closer. His tongue began doing crazy things to my right ear, sending warmth through my entire body. It was almost as if my body called to him. I tried to pull back. The beach, the body-calling crap, it was all a huge cliché, and yet I couldn't stop it.

I lost the tenuous control I had and my arms wrapped around his neck. *You shouldn't do this. It isn't right.* There was still part of my brain hanging on to sanity.

"Let go," he whispered.

"It's only a dream." I took a deep breath and let it out. So what was the harm in letting go? No one would ever know but me.

I looked around and saw that we were alone on the beach.

"I want you," he growled. The sound sent zinging sensations through me and made my body hum with need.

I couldn't think of anything sexy to say as he was now nibbling the sensitive parts of my neck, making me gasp with pleasure. His tongue slid down between my breasts and I wasn't sure how much longer I'd be able to stand.

The second I thought it, we suddenly tumbled to the ground and I landed on top of him. His hardness swelled beneath me and it gave me power. *He wants me.*

"Yes." His hands tangled in my hair, he brought my face to his and kissed me. Not a tentative getting-to-know-you thing, but a kiss with hard-core passion.

I melted. I couldn't keep my hips from writhing against

him. My thong was no barrier and I felt his heat. As I moved against him, he brought his thumb up and began teasing the most sensitive part of my body. I needed release and he matched my motions. In seconds I climaxed. "Arath," I whispered into his mouth, feeling as though I'd just experienced some kind of incredible connection.

Music played and it became louder and louder. "What is that?"

"I believe you call it Fall Out Boy." Arath smiled. "Time to go, Guardian. Enjoy your day."

"No!" I screamed in frustration. "I don't want the dream to end."

"Who says it is a dream? I can live in all realities." His voice and his image faded away, leaving me on my knees in the sand.

I sat straight up in bed expecting to see him, but he wasn't there. The phone rang. Reaching out a hand, I picked it up. "This better be good." The song by Fall Out Boy was the music I'd designated on my phone for Claire.

"Hmmm. Hello, Miss Cranky Pants. I must have interrupted a really great dream." Claire laughed on the other end.

My skin was still hot from the encounter. "You know that sleep isn't easy for me to get these days. What's up?"

"I haven't heard from Bailey. He was going to come to Fiji after the charity ball. We're having some trouble with one of the cameras."

"Okay, and this is my problem because…?" Sleep still clouded my brain. "Sorry, that came out testier than I meant."

"It's okay. You're never very nice when we wake you up. I can't get ahold of Alex or Mira. They are both doing Guardian stuff. I've got to go underwater in a bit and I just needed to talk to Bailey about the camera. I've been trying to find him since last night. He was at the house, but I missed him when I went for the fitting. He'd already taken a plane to Houston to see some friends of his. He's not answering his phone."

"Claire, I'm not Bailey's keeper. You know that. Besides, if he's in Houston there's a really good chance he's passed out on someone's couch. Those NASA guys know how to party. Remember the last time. He threw up for four days after their tequila *Star Wars* marathon." I glanced at the clock on my nightstand. I had two hours before I had to get ready to do a local morning talk show. It was one of the many ways we were promoting the ball.

I didn't mind television; we'd been in front of cameras most of our lives. We'd talk about what kind of champagne and food would be served. Who would show up on the red carpet and what I might wear. Silly and necessary, I only hoped they didn't bring up the stupid rumors about Emilio.

"I'll get Jake to check into it, and I'll make sure he calls you today. Be careful on your dive, and I'm sorry for being so grumpy this morning. I need a big cup of coffee."

She laughed. "That's the truth. I'll see you tonight, and don't worry. It will be a beautiful event. It always is."

To be honest, I hadn't obsessed over the ball like I usually did, probably because the whole destruction of the universe played a heavier role right now. As soon as I hung up the phone it rang again. This time it was Georgia.

"I know you've been busy with, um, stuff. Kathy Tracy at the ABC affiliate called and wanted to know if you'd be there this morning."

"Call her back and tell her I'll be there in about an hour. Is Jax meeting me there to do makeup?"

"Yep. And I'm not supposed to tell you this, but she says she has some heavy-duty concealer just in case. Last time your dark circles took half a pound of makeup."

I laughed hard at that. That time, I'd been on a three-day demon-killing binge when I had to make a sudden appearance on the red carpet at the Kodak Theatre in Hollywood. It was Oscar night and one of Claire's documentaries had been nominated. She didn't win, but we all wanted to be there for her.

I had sat down in the makeup chair in a suite at the Renaissance Hotel next door to the theater, and Jax had actually gasped. I told her if she could make me look decent there was an extra five hundred in it for her. She told me to keep my money. If she could make me look good, she would consider it her greatest masterpiece. Even I couldn't believe the face in the mirror when she'd finished. It had been that good. We'd been friends ever since and anytime I had a big event I flew her out to wherever I was.

"She's already there. Says the coffee's crap so bring her something decent."

"Okay. I'll call when we're done. I promise I'll do my best to make it in. I know the paperwork is piling up."

"Eh. It's been worse." Georgia laughed before she hung up.

Jax wasn't any better than me without a decent cup of coffee. I decided I better fill a thermos for the both of us.

"There." Jax put the finishing touches on my makeup. "You look like the diva you are." She was short, maybe five feet if that, and one of the most beautiful women I'd ever met. Her heritage was a mix of Asian and Irish, and the result was an extraordinary beauty.

"Hey, what did you do to your knees? Maybe I should put some cover-up on those." She reached for a bigger brush and I looked down to see that both of my knees had rug burns. No, not a rug—sand burns.

My hand flew to my mouth, but I caught myself before I gasped. "No telling with me. Must have done something during my workout last night. I was so tired this morning I didn't even notice."

It can't be. It was a dream.

Kristen Crane stuck her head in just as I stood up. "I'm so glad you could make it in this morning. We always have fun." She shook my hand. "I just want you to know that I talked to Kathy. We aren't going to throw you any curveballs today. I saw what happened the other day at the press conference and was appalled. Markie was a friend of mine, too, and I won't let anyone drag her name in the mud."

"Thank you." I smiled. "I wouldn't expect you to pull any punches, but I appreciate you letting me know beforehand. I still get a little teary-eyed when someone mentions her, and I really don't want to take away from our kids. She wouldn't want that either."

Kristen nodded. She was the opposite of Jax, a blonde Amazon. "Agreed. But I warn you: I will be drilling you on what you're going to wear tonight. That seems to be the big buzz this morning. Did you see the poll on *E!*? Their website shows that sixty percent of the people think you're going to show up in a black dress."

I laughed. It was crazy the things people were interested in when it came to "celebrities." "You can drill me about the dress all you want, but I still haven't made up my mind which one I'm going to wear tonight."

"Well, then we'll talk about that. See you out there."

As the interview ended, Kristen gave it one last try. "Please, our viewers want to know which dress you picked." She leaned forward expectantly. When she shifted her position, I noticed someone in the shadows behind her.

Arath.

Until that moment, the interview had gone off without a hitch.

I gave a slight cough and took a sip from the glass of water beside me. I gave her my best smile. "You and the viewers will find out tonight, and don't forget to make those donations on the 800 number."

Kristen gave the number again and signed off.

"You were terrific, as always." Taking my hands, she kissed my cheek. "I'll see you this evening."

After saying a quick good-bye to Jax, I motioned for Arath to follow me out to the car. I tried to keep my patience, but it was difficult. He climbed into the passenger seat and I started the car.

"Guardian, what are you doing?"

"I'm driving, *King Arath*. I thought you were going to message ahead from now on."

It wasn't hard to notice how he had trouble fitting into the seat. The Mercedes was lux, but it wasn't built for a man his size. "You need to put your seat belt on."

He stared blankly. "The restraints?" I pointed to the belt. "You bring it around your chest and fasten it there." I pointed down to the buckle.

It took him a few tries, but he finally managed it. "I did tell your people I was here. Your phone was off, so they could not alert you."

"So you just showed up at an interview where there were cameras? How did you get past the station security?"

"I made sure they were distracted and walked past. I also made certain to stay in the shadows so that no one but you saw me."

"I hope you're right, because I really don't want to have to explain you. Hey—wait a minute. How did you get through? The portals are closed."

"The mages on the council have opened one gate to Earth that is protected by magic."

Mom had mentioned that the night before, but I'd been so busy I'd forgotten.

"Tell me again, why are you here? The last time we spoke you shoved me into a Vex tunnel because your world was being overrun by black magic."

"The immediate threat is over, though the darkness still pervades. I'm sure your mother told you that several worlds are involved. What I have discovered on my planet is that there is unity within the darkness. I believe you call it a cult or society of some sort. These people work quietly to bring the evil into our worlds. And they are here, as the portals the other day were opened from this side."

I looked at the roof of the car for a brief moment. *Why does this have to happen today?* There was so much to do before the ball, and making sure this event happened would take every bit of energy I had. It might sound selfish, but the universe could wait.

"Is there a reason my presence here causes you distress?"

I shoved the car into gear and backed out. "No." *Yes.* The dream flashed through my mind. Oh, jeez. *Get it together, Gilly.*

It was hard not to smile when I noticed Arath white-knuckling the dash. "Is this your first ride in a car?"

"Does it normally go so fast?" The heater kicked in and he jumped when the warm air blew out of the vents.

I had to laugh. "Yes, especially when I'm driving. Do you have any idea who this cult is?"

"Unfortunately, those on my planet preferred to die rather than tell me the truth. Their minds were protected by the evil, so it was no use reading them."

Die? He really did have an interesting way of doing business.

"Well, perhaps we can do some investigating on this side to see what we can find out. Maybe one of the mages can trace the magic."

Arath was silent. I glanced over at him and his eyes were closed as if he were concentrating.

"Are you okay?"

"I must return to Maunra. There is trouble at the castle again."

"How can you do that?"

"I am attuned to my people. They need me. Can you please stop the machine?"

I nodded. "Give me just a second and I'll find a place to pull over." We needed a space where he could disappear without anyone seeing. Since we were less than a mile from the office, I pulled into the private parking garage there and shut the automatic door behind us. "You should be safe here."

It took him a moment to find the door handle and release his seat belt. "Be safe, Guardian," he said as he stepped onto the concrete floor. Then he was gone.

Bye.

Kristen had been true to her word earlier about not asking obnoxious questions. I wished I could say the same about the rest of the press.

I did a series of phone interviews for radio and print from my downtown office. Most of the reporters were respectful, but a couple brought up the question of Emilio and Markie and I deflected it as well as I could. I was always trying to bring the topic back to art and the kids we wanted to help. It wasn't easy.

One reporter in particular, from a radio station in San Antonio, kept bringing up Markie. I didn't lose my temper, but I was firm. "I don't know how you feel about your friends, but Markie just died and I don't appreciate people trying to create some kind of scandal out of it. It was tragic and very sad, and quite frankly my heart still hurts." I sniffled. "We're going on with this event because Markie loved these kids as much as I do. She was passionate about art and she loved life. It isn't fair that someone took hers, but don't you dare try to sully her name with scandal. She was a wonderful, caring woman, and I will miss her more than you know."

There was a few seconds of dead air. "Thanks for taking the

time with us, Ms. Caruthers, and good luck with the event."
Then there was a dial tone.

I laughed. "Guess he wasn't ready for the truth."

Sighing, I picked up the phone again to check my messages.
Kyle had called with the discovery that Markie had bought one
of Emilio's paintings from the Paris gallery I own. The trans-
action had taken place over the phone. It wasn't unusual for her
to buy a piece and tell me about it later, but it was strange that
she'd bought it the day she was murdered.

If Emilio was in any way involved with her, I'd have to kill
him, especially if he had anything to do with her death.

CHAPTER

18

Before I knew it, the time to get ready for the Arts in Schools Ball had arrived. I'd spent most of the day promoting the event while catching up on paperwork at the office.

As I headed home Kyle called with news about the murders. The medical examiners couldn't identify one of the toxins found in both victims. That made me wonder if magic might be involved. The murders had been almost identical in that their hearts were cut out and weird incisions had been made on the palms of their hands. With the question about the magic, there was a good chance the killer or killers might not be of the human variety.

"Weird thing is," Kyle told me as he waited for his flight back to Texas from New York, "the fibers under Markie's fingernails also can't be identified. We thought at first it might be the carpet from the motel, but it isn't. Looks like she may have fought with the killer before he shot her with whatever drugs he was using. But there's no DNA, just the weird material."

I would have liked to think over what he had said, but it was now two hours before the event, and I still hadn't decided on a dress.

Time to focus.

Jax had already put the final touches on my makeup, leaving me a couple of tubes of lipstick depending on the dress I chose. She went back to her hotel to dress and then she'd be available at the party for touch-ups should anyone need them. It wasn't unusual to have a hairdresser, stylist, and makeup artist in the sidelines, especially before going up onstage in front of hundreds of people.

I wasn't as high maintenance as some celebs, not that I ever really thought of myself that way. But with the Caruthers sisters always on the prowl for bad guys, we never knew which one of us might show up at party needing a major overhaul.

In front of my mirror I contemplated one of the three dresses Alex had picked out for me. The first had been a red sequined number that fit me perfectly, but I just wasn't in a red kind of mood. Maybe it was all the dreams about blood lately.

I liked the second one, which was a slinky black concoction from Calvin Klein. I thought about the poll on *E!* and picked up the third dress. A silver piece of fabulosity that looked as if it had been sewn by fairies.

Mo barked his approval from the ottoman and I reached down to pet his head.

"I like it, too, buddy." The dress fit my body perfectly. Ethereal and flowing, it made me feel like a princess.

"I knew it." Alex poked her head in the door. "We need to put your hair up. Nothing too fancy, but it will show off that draped neckline."

"You made it. Is everything okay?" I turned to see the rear view. The dress dipped to my lower back, but not so far as to be crude.

"It's not great, but there's been a lull in the action. I have time to put in an appearance, but I may not be able to stay for the entire gala."

"Are you going to tell me what happened with Ginjin the other day? You two seemed mighty cozy."

Rolling her eyes, she poked me with her finger. "Basically, I pulled him to safety. I just happened to land in the right spot at the right time. His wing had been ripped to shreds. He wasn't pleased, which is so typical. He told me, 'I was prepared for death.'" She used a silly macho accent. "I told him that his chance for martyrdom would have to wait another day because his people needed him."

I laughed. "Considering your history with him, I have to admit I'm surprised you didn't leave him to die."

She smirked. "I'm still wondering about that myself. Nothing's really changed, except that he hasn't tried to kill me in the last twenty-four hours. Of course, we've both been busy protecting the mages so they can work their spells. When I left, things had settled down considerably."

I glanced in the mirror at the gown she'd picked out for me. "I don't know how you do it. One minute you're pulling dragons out of the fire, the next you're my own personal stylist."

Alex rummaged through one of the drawers in my closet and pulled out some bobby pins and two diamond-encrusted combs. "It's a gift. Besides, it's no different from your killing a horde of demons and then showing up on the red carpet an hour later." She laughed as she came out, her hands full with items for my hair. Her gown was deep sapphire, her signature color. "I saw your dress in Paris this fall, and knew when it walked down the runway it was made for you. I saved it for tonight."

"Then why the other dresses?"

"You always like choices. If I'd given you just the one dress, you would have wondered if something else might have worked better."

Damn. She knew me too well. "I love it." I air-kissed her cheek, as we were both made up to the nines.

"Sit down so I can fix your hair." She pointed to the chair.

I spread out the skirt and sat down in front of the vanity. In a matter of seconds she'd whipped my hair into a loose chignon and placed the diamond combs in the back. "You look beautiful, as always." She smiled.

"So do you."

"Well, I'm off to make sure everything is in place. The limo will be here at seven thirty to pick up you and Claire. Mira and Bailey are arriving on their own."

Bailey. Crap. I'd forgotten all about Claire's request.

"If I haven't said it in the last twenty minutes, thank you again for pulling all this together. Do you have any idea how many millions of dollars we're going to raise? We'll have art and music programs in every school in Texas. Then maybe we can take on the rest of the world."

Alex took my hand. "Hey, the Caruthers are always here for one another, and you forget, art is one of my passions, too. It is a work of love. I just can't wait for you to see what we did." She glanced down at the diamond watch on her wrist. "Gotta go."

I followed not far behind in search of Claire. She was in her room, which was pink and white. Out of the four girls, she's the least froufrou of the bunch, but she loves pink.

I found her cross-legged on her bed with a pile of books. "Hey, *chica*, it's almost time for us to go. You need to get dressed."

She held out a finger indicating she needed a second.

"Do you want to meet me downstairs?"

"No, hold on." She still didn't look up.

I sat in one of the white fluffy chairs waiting for her, grateful my dress wouldn't show wrinkles. Whatever she was reading, it must have been fascinating. She couldn't take her eyes from the page. Claire looked like a surfer girl, but she had a brain like no other. The only person I knew close to her intelligence was our brother, Bailey. He was great with gadgets and anything electronic, but Claire could absorb anything.

Finally she took her nose out of the book. "You aren't going to believe this." She closed the tome she'd been perusing. Her hazel eyes were bright with excitement. "Your demon king isn't a demon."

"Did you sniff glue today? What the hell are you talking about?" I frowned at her.

She sat on the edge of the bed, her long, tanned legs slipping out from under her robe. "I can't be sure, but I think he's one hundred percent mage. From what you described, only a real mage could do something like send you through a Vex, or close not just his portals, but ones all over the universe. This has been bugging me all day. I cut my location search short and skipped my hunky man breakfast to come back here and do research.

"Think about it, Gilly. What you saw weren't just the portals going from his world to ours. You were closing portals to other dimensions. The whole thing is mind-boggling."

"Claire, there has to be some other explanation. I saw him go all demon, big and red with fangs." I did the international sign for long canines with my fingers. "He turned one of his own people into a pile of ashes before I could blink. He's definitely demon. Maybe you missed something."

"I don't think so. Do you have any idea how rare male mages like him are? There's one born every one hundred years or so. They have incredible powers. They can travel through time and space with a word. They control minds, and have enough power to close portals without being a Guardian. We'd have to confirm it with Mom, but it makes sense from what I've read."

"But we know who his father was, so he has to be at least half demon."

Claire stepped into her pink evening gown and turned so that I could zip up the back. "Screwy genetics and I'm sure it has something to do with the fact that Arath and his brother are twins. I haven't made it that far in the research." She slipped on a pair of bright pink Manolos that matched her dress perfectly, and faced me. "His father may be demon, but who knows what happens when a mage mates with a demon. As far as I can tell Aunt Juliet was the first."

My brain hurt from trying to understand what she said. Oh, it wasn't that difficult, but the idea that Arath wasn't a demon, or at least partly so, was preposterous. "But why, and did she know what she was doing? I can't believe she would knowingly leave her children on Maunra to be raised by a beast. Mom made it sound like Aunt Juliet had no idea Arath and Throe were alive. She told me specifically to keep my mouth shut about it."

Claire shrugged. "That's where you come in. We definitely need to do some investigating."

I blew out a breath. "Aunt Juliet better show at the fund-raiser tonight. I don't think I can stand the suspense much longer."

Smiling, Claire led me out the door. "If anyone can find out what's going on, it's the Caruthers sisters."

CHAPTER
19

Alex never failed to get A-listers to a party she gave. So it was no surprise that everywhere I turned I bumped into a celebrity at the Arts in Schools Ball.

She'd turned the venue into an ethereal fairyland. Using a secret garden theme, the place was filled with every flower imaginable. Their scent, mixed with hundreds of vanilla votives, made it intoxicating. The lighting had been situated so that there were brighter places for people to visit and dine, and then the dance floor and bar areas were cozy and intimate.

The entire building had been tented with filmy pale fabrics, hiding any indication that it was an airplane hangar. It was November so she had a few heating posts strewn throughout the building to keep away the chill. Everything was absolutely perfect, and the place was packed.

After spending nearly an hour on the red carpet, and saying a few hellos to friends, I went in search of my sister so I could tell her what a wonderful job she'd done. I also wanted to know if she'd seen Aunt Juliet.

At the bar I picked up a glass of champagne. A quick sip and my shoulders relaxed. I moved toward the tables to the left of the bandstand, which held a seventeen-piece orchestra.

"Please forgive me, *bella*," Emilio's silken voice said from behind me.

The sound of his voice made my spine stiffen involuntarily. I thought about walking off, but I knew he'd follow. I had to face him. Dressed in a tuxedo, he exuberated Italian heat. It was no wonder I'd wanted him, but not anymore.

"What are you doing here?" I sounded cold, even to me, but he didn't deserve more.

"I came to see you. I can't stand being without you, my love. You're so beautiful." He reached out to touch my cheek with his fingers and I stepped back.

"Emilio, you shouldn't have wasted your time. I said everything I had to say at the gallery. I'll represent your work, but I no longer want anything to do with you on a personal level."

"You are still angry, but I know you still feel the passion for me, as I do you." As if to prove his point, he touched my arm. "We were good together, and we can be again. I only want your forgiveness."

The absurdity of the situation hadn't escaped me. "You cheated with one of my employees in my home. Maybe that is acceptable behavior where you come from, but it isn't for me." We were beginning to draw interested looks from the people at the bar. "And you had to have seen the gossip rags linking you to Markie. If I find out it's true, you'll have a lot more than my anger to deal with, and if you don't let go of my arm right now you'll find out just how strong I am."

"Gillian, you cannot believe I would have had anything to do with your friend." He waved his hand as he let go of me. "It is horrible what happened to her, but it has nothing to do with me."

"For your sake, you better be telling the truth." I stared him down. "If I discover any hint that you had something to do with what happened to Markie, your life will be in serious jeopardy. I promise you that."

He had the good grace to look appalled. "You are obviously upset and aren't thinking clearly. Why don't I get us something to drink and we can chat somewhere privately?"

I almost growled. "It's time for you to leave, Emilio. This night is important to me, and I won't let you destroy it."

As I tried to make my graceful exit, I slammed into a hard chest.

Arath was dressed in a tuxedo looking like something that just stepped out of *Men's Vogue*. His eyes were on me.

Emilio had his hand on my shoulder, and Arath lifted it off. "I believe *my date* asked you to leave her alone." He said the words with a smile, the menace implied.

177

"Your date?" Emilio squeaked. His normally suave voice sounded pained. I pulled my eyes away from Arath to see what had happened.

Emilio was holding one hand in the other, which meant Arath had definitely applied some pressure.

I crooked my arm into Arath's. I felt shocked that he was here in the middle of my charity ball, and incredibly grateful at the same time. "I wondered where you were." I stood on my tiptoes to kiss his cheek and suddenly my lips were on his. He'd turned his face so that he could capture a kiss, and I gave it to him.

Warmth spilled through my body as his hands slid to my lower back and pressed me into him. More than warmth, fire. It took me a few seconds to remember where we were.

I cleared my throat. "Later, darling," I whispered.

Emilio didn't say anything. The anger burned in his eyes as he stomped past us, still cradling his hand.

I couldn't help but laugh. "I don't know what the hell you're doing here, but thank you."

"He was right about one thing, you are beautiful." Before it slipped from my hands, he took my glass of champagne away and set it up on the bar. "I suppose he is one of your many spurned lovers?" It wasn't an accusation, more an observation.

"He was the one who did the spurning, if there is such a thing. Not that I'm not grateful for the save, but what are you doing here?"

"I have something to discuss with you." He put his hand

around my waist and led me away from the crowd at the bar. "We should dance." He pulled me into a slow waltz before I could respond. We made it to the corner of the dance floor before my brain kicked into gear.

"How do you know the waltz?"

His left eyebrow arched and his head tilted to the right. "You are not the only beings who enjoy dancing."

Well, okay then. "I hate to spoil your fun but I've been to many celebrations in your world and not once have I seen anyone dance."

"I've been studying Earth for a very long time. And—"

"What?"

"I watch the DVDs of *Dancing with the Stars*. It is a most interesting show."

I chuckled. "I wasn't aware that you watched television on Maunra."

"There are many things you do not know about my world." The music changed and he slowed the pace. The parts of my body pressed into his began to hum.

Focus, Gillian.

We glided across the floor as if we'd been doing it for ages. "Are you going to tell me why you're here?"

His hand caressed my cheek and I resisted the urge to lay my head on his chest.

"Enjoy the dance, Gillian." He said my name as if it were velvet, and it bothered me that I was excited. Being so close to him sent my body into overdrive.

I had so many questions and things I felt I should tell him. Like that his mother was still alive. There had never been a good time. And maybe, just maybe, I didn't want to open a can of worms until I understood what was going on a little better. Aunt Juliet had been away on council business since I found out. And I felt that I should talk to her before even thinking about telling Arath what I knew.

I couldn't quite bring myself to say, "Arath, you're not a demon. Did you know that? And, um, your mother is alive."

I was so enamored with my dance partner that it took me a moment to realize the music had stopped. He guided me off the dance floor.

"Your phone is about to ring. Tell them the problem has been taken care of, and there is no need to worry."

My cell buzzed inside my diamond-encrusted, star-shaped Judith Leiber purse. Jake was on the other line with news that two demons had jumped in. "One of them has gone off the grid. The other one is near your location."

"The situation has been handled, Jake. Thanks." I hung up the phone and addressed Arath. "How did you know that? What's going on?" The strap had slipped on my heel and I lifted my leg to put it back on. Arath watched as the dress slid up to my knee. His eyes briefly flashed orange and then back. Knowing I was attractive to him gave me a secret thrill.

"There's someone on this side helping the Krod clan plan a coup."

"Um, excuse me?"

"The reason you've had so much trouble lately is because someone on this side is working against us both."

"Okay, you told me that earlier. Did you find out who? And how would someone here be able to help your world? It doesn't make any sense."

He shook his head. "It has something to do with weapons and trade, but I did not discover the source. Mond of the Krod clan discovered me following him, and I killed him in battle before getting the answers I desired. I do know that it involves your family. There is an assassination plot. I was able to decipher that much. Someone, perhaps you, or your sisters, are in danger."

I shrugged. "Oh. Honestly, that's nothing new. There's always someone trying to kill one of us. It's a part of being a Guardian."

"Perhaps, but I thought it best to make sure you were aware of the situation." He looked over my shoulder. His eyes went from a very human brown to a bright yellow, and then flashed back. I turned to see what had caused the change.

Aunt Juliet. Oh, crap.

CHAPTER

20

"I, um. That's a very close friend of my family. Are you hungry?" I tried to steer him away from her to the piles of shrimp and lobster. "Or, you know, I could use a little air. We can go outside and you can tell me more about this assassination plot." I tugged on his arm, but he dug in his heels.

I turned to see Aunt Juliet approaching. *This is really, really bad.*

"Gillian, darling," she said as she kissed both of my cheeks. "Who is this handsome devil?"

Her comment made me cough.

I had no idea how to respond. He looked at Aunt Juliet as if he knew who she was. It couldn't be possible. She hadn't seen her children since they were babies.

He reached out a hand. "I am Arath, Gillian's date for the evening."

In an automatic movement she reached out her hand, and when their skin touched her eyes flashed to his face. "Oh," was all she said as she fainted.

Arath caught her and carried her out one of the side doors and we found a small office in the hangar with a couch. Carefully placing her on the sofa, he turned to me. "Did you know?"

My mouth and brain couldn't get it together.

"Did you know she was my mother?" Anger tinged his voice, but he didn't bellow like he usually did.

"How—I mean, yes and no. I had an idea," I stammered.

"I do not understand." His frown deepened.

"I don't either," I confessed. "You told me that your mother was dead. I came back and checked. You can imagine my surprise when her name"—I pointed to Juliet—"was attached to yours. I thought it some clerical error. And I haven't had a chance to talk to her about it. She's been gone for weeks, and my father is dead, so there just wasn't anyone else."

That wasn't exactly true. My mother could have helped, but she chose not to. I didn't want to get into that with Arath. "I'm not sure, but from the paperwork I saw, I think she thought you were dead. That's probably why she fainted."

He crossed his arms across his chest as he stared at her. "She did think I was dead."

"How do you know that?"

"I read her mind. She knew by the touch of my skin who I was. She loved me."

"Of course she did. Wait—you read her mind?"

His eyebrow rose.

Before I could even think *Oh, crap*, Aunt Juliet stirred. "Um, maybe you should stand by the door. We don't want to give her another shock just yet."

He nodded and moved away.

I sat on the couch and took the older woman's hands in mine. Her eyes fluttered open.

"Are you okay?" I squeezed her fingers and smiled at her reassuringly.

"I—where is my son?" She sat up.

I looked over at Arath, and she turned so she could see him. Tears streamed down her cheeks and she sobbed.

"They told me you died." She shook her hands free of mine and reached to him. "All this time I thought you were dead."

For more than a minute an array of emotions crossed his face. He was no more certain of the situation than Juliet. His feet were planted, his arms behind his back. He watched her hands as she continued to reach for him, and then finally took them in his own.

I let out the breath I'd been holding.

She touched his cheek. "Your father said you and Throe had been killed during a raid. They had taken you from me, and insisted you be raised on Maunra. It was the best place for you to learn the magic that would protect you. We knew the day you were born that you had incredible power. Back then, the evil was as prevalent as it is now, and Earth was not safe for you." The words tumbled out of her mouth in a rush, her cheeks slowly growing pink in color.

"I was promised visitation rights every two weeks. For the first month everything went as planned. I didn't like it, but I cherished those four days with you. I knew from the day you were born that you were both going to be very special."

Kissing his hands, she continued. "When they told me what had happened, I couldn't bear it. You were meant for something beyond what any of the rest of us were capable, my son, and I could not believe the universe had lost someone so special. And my babies—it was just too much. I didn't even question it. No one would do that to a mother."

Arath's jaw tightened. "My father always spoke of you with reverence, but he saw our human side as a weakness."

I remembered the vision of Arath and his brother being shaken by their father. It must have been the truth. That kind of life could not have been easy for someone like Arath, who had a compassionate side, as well as the warrior within him.

"He was a stubborn fool, and while I don't like to speak ill of the dead, I hope he's burning in the fires of hell for what he did to us. Your talent for magic came from me, and it makes you a formidable foe. Am I right?"

He nodded. "My father was an honorable man; I cannot understand his deception."

Juliet sighed. "I wish I didn't but I do. In his own way

he protected you. He knew that you wouldn't be safe in my world. As you know, demons aren't welcome on Earth, and it was a turbulent time here. We were in the middle of a war between good and evil." She stopped and looked up at the ceiling as if that would help stem the tears. "Do you know how I met him?"

"No. We weren't allowed to ask anything about you. Our father spoke of you on occasion, perhaps three times that I can remember."

This time her small smile was sad. "I'm a mage, and at that time worked as a Guardian. I was in your world helping with the spells to bind the portals. There had been a shift between worlds, much like what is happening now, and I'd been sent to ward your planet. Your father was my protector during my time there. He was a charismatic man. He didn't much care for me in the beginning, but I think I eventually charmed him.

"I slipped and we shared a dream one night. Dreams are only one of the many realities in which a mage can live. I'll spare you the details, but it was a passionate one. A month later I discovered I was pregnant. I'd returned to Earth, and decided I would raise you here. But when you were born those beautiful eyes of yours burned orange, and I knew you wouldn't be safe until you were able to control your powers.

"Gillian's father helped me work out an agreement with your father, who was pleased that he had two sons. He never gave any indication that he didn't care for the human part of your DNA. He loved you from the first moment he saw you and Throe.

"It was no safer for me on your planet than it was for you here, and my presence could have brought harm to your father and you. The arrangement worked for that first month, and then he came to see me one night. He told me that you had been killed in a raid. He was so upset, and I had no reason not to believe him. Devastated, I never could return to Maunra. If warding needed to be done, another mage took my place."

Arath and Aunt Juliet sat in silence for several moments.

"Is your brother—where is Throe?"

"He's in the Malan dimension setting up trade agreements. He will be pleased to know our mother lives."

They continued to stare at one another.

I cleared my throat. "I should probably get back to the party before my sisters begin to wonder what happened, and I'm supposed to give a short speech. I'm sure you have so much to say to one another. Take your time."

Juliet stopped me as I walked to the door. "Gillian, please find my date, Signor Batolli. He's a handsome man with a gray streak going through his black hair. Very distinguished, and a lovely Italian accent. Alex knows him."

I grabbed the doorknob. "Sure, no problem." I left them to get reacquainted.

The ballroom was even more crowded than when I'd left. I found Alex checking on the silent auction items. "Gilly, where have you been?" Dressed in Chanel couture, with her hair in an updo, she was the picture of the perfect socialite. If only these people knew what she really did for a living.

"Busy visiting. It looks like you have another smashing success on your hands. What's the bid on the Canyon Ranch package?" I wanted to distract her from asking any more questions about where I'd been.

Mira walked over. With her green dress and red hair she was nothing less than stunning. Claire was right behind her, looking fashionably young and chic.

We stood in a small circle. "Damn, we look good." Mira laughed. "That silver looks hot on you, Gilly."

I smiled. "Thanks."

"Who was the guy you were dancing with?" Claire asked. "That's all anyone is talking about. Someone saw him duke it out with Emilio at the bar and then kiss you."

Amazing how rumors started. Before I could answer she continued.

"And why did Aunt Juliet faint when she saw him? I mean, he's beyond hot, but she actually passed out from touching him."

I coughed, not certain how to answer. "It's Arath."

There was a collective gasp as the implications dawned on them. "Wait, Arath. As in the demon king?" Alex whispered so that those around us couldn't hear.

"Yes. He was here chasing down a demon." I looked around and discovered we were attracting attention. "Someone is trying to work a deal to help with a coup, and one of us is in danger. He didn't have all the details, but it looks like another assassination attempt against one of us."

My sisters nodded. "Will everyone be back at the house tonight?" Mira asked. "I feel like we should have one of our sisterly powwows. I could use a good power infusion."

When the four of us meditated together we were able to share and build our power. It was much like recharging a battery.

"I'm headed back to Fiji," said Claire. "We start filming the tiger shark migration on Tuesday. I've already scouted out some of the spots."

"Ack. I forgot about my meetings in New York, so I'm heading out on a red-eye tonight," Mira added. "We'll have to get together soon, but you better message us and tell us what's going on."

"I will. Now, my lovely sisters, you go out among the crowd and get them to open up those checkbooks. These silent-auction numbers aren't nearly as high as I would like."

I couldn't keep from wondering what Juliet and Arath were talking about, but I was sure they needed more time. Heck, they'd need years to get to know one another again. Alex pointed out Signor Batolli to me, and I introduced myself.

"It's a pleasure to meet you, Miss Caruthers. Juliet speaks kindly of your family." She was right about him being handsome, in an elderly gentleman way. I reached out to shake his hand, but he didn't take it.

He bowed his head instead. "My apologies for not taking your hand, I've been suffering from a cold."

Odd, since I saw no sign of a red nose or sniffling. *He must be taking one heck of a cold medicine.* There was something about him, in his eyes, as if he knew important things I didn't. It bugged the hell out of me. Maybe it was that he had that air of a wise old gentleman who'd seen a bit too much of the world.

"My aunt asked me to let you know she's been detained by business, but she'll be back soon."

"That is good news." He gave a short smile and glanced around the room. "She sent me for champagne and then I lost her."

"The business was—very sudden. Have you had a chance to view the auction items? Alex procured a Bentley for the cause, and the last bid I saw was very low." I motioned him toward the tables in the back of the room.

He bowed toward me. "Again, a pleasure to meet you, my dear."

I nodded to him.

"Have a wonderful evening."

My speech wasn't far off, so I decided to spruce up in the hair and makeup room. I caught up with Aunt Juliet there as she repaired her makeup.

I touched her shoulder and she patted my hand. There were too many women around to say much. "Is everything okay?" I whispered.

"Yes, he's a lovely boy. He asked me to tell you he had to go. There's trouble"—she looked around—"at work."

I smiled. "No problem. I didn't want to have to explain him to the gossip mavens."

I needed her to know that I wanted to tell her the truth days ago. She'd always been beyond kind to me, a second mother. The one person I could go to when the chips were really down and I didn't want my family to know what a loser I was.

"I'm sorry I didn't prepare you. I've known for a while. At least, I knew something. You and Mom have been gone for weeks, and it wasn't the kind of thing I could message you about. I feel awful. For both of you."

She squeezed my hand. "It's all right, darling. It was a shock. There is so much more to the story, but this isn't the place." She indicated some rather nosy women putting on several layers of lipstick.

"Well, your date is waiting for you," I told her. "I'm afraid I steered him to the auction tables, as our numbers are falling a little short this evening. May I ask where you met him?"

"In Cannes last year. He happened to be in the States for business this week and flew here tonight. This is only my second date with him, but he's a very charming man, and a wonderful companion."

We all knew what she meant by "companion." It was a gentler word for lover. The idea of Signor Batolli and Juliet going at it was not a visual I needed in my head.

"What kind of business is he in?"

She turned back to me. "My, you're a curious girl. Do you have a crush on my date?"

I laughed. "No. He was just so interesting." I couldn't tell her that he had a weird vibe. She'd been through enough, and I didn't want to hurt her feelings.

She patted my arm. "To be honest, dear, I don't really know. I believe it's something to do with investment banking. He's also quite the collector. Art, homes, I think he even owns an island or two."

I followed her out and watched as she met her date. He smiled at her and took her in his arms, but I noticed the smile didn't reach his eyes.

Biting my lip, I went in search of Alex to see what she knew about Juliet's new man. There was something about him that didn't seem right, and I couldn't help being overprotective. She and I both had a homing device for jerks. If I could save her some heartache later on, it was worth a bit of snooping now.

Before I could find Alex, Georgia, my assistant, pulled on my arm. "I'm sorry to bother you, but it's time for you to give your speech." She handed me a small slip of paper, and her hand was shaking so badly she almost dropped it.

"Hey, what's wrong?"

She ducked her head. "It's nothing. I think my imagination is getting the best of me." Georgia was competent and not one to give in to flights of fancy.

"Please, tell me what's bothering you. Is it the ball? You and Alex have done a wonderful job, but I know we've overworked you. Do you need to go home? I can certainly handle the rest of the evening."

She gave me a quick smile. "I promise, it's nothing. I just

had a weird feeling on my way here this afternoon. Like, I don't know, someone was watching me." Looking up, she shrugged. "It's so silly, but I ran from the car into the hangar this afternoon. No one but the caterer was here, and, oh, I don't know. It gave me chills. And I keep having the same sensation. I look over my shoulder but no one is there."

Given the recent murders I didn't take the news lightly. We hadn't told the employees about Reuben yet, as the police were still trying to find his next of kin.

"Georgia, I don't think it's silly at all. Promise when you are ready to go home that you'll take my limo. There's been a lot of weird stuff going on lately. Tell the driver I said to walk you to your door and let him search throughout the house. I'm going to call my friend Kyle. You know him, the detective. He'll probably have some questions about anything weird you might have seen, or if you noticed something out of place the last few days."

"That's too much trouble." She twisted the sleeve of her dress, so I knew she was nervous. All of this seemed very out of character for her. "It's not necessary. I'm sure it's just my overactive imagination."

I hugged her. "It's purely selfishness on my part. I refuse to let anything happen to you. How in the world would I survive without you? You are also a dear friend. So take the limo and we'll both feel better."

Taking a deep breath, she smiled. "Thank you, but how will you get home?"

"I'll ride with one of my sisters, or Bailey. Hey, have you seen him lately?"

"No, his flight came in a couple of hours ago from Houston, but he hasn't been checked off the list at the door."

"Knowing Bailey, he's still in Houston. They'll have to throw him out of the place to get rid of him."

The lights dimmed and Alex was spotlighted on the stage. The music stopped, and the crowd hushed to a whisper.

"Time for me to get these people to open up those wallets." I smiled at Georgia.

CHAPTER

21

The ball finally ended at two, and my sisters and I were the last to leave. We all piled into Alex's limo, exhausted but happy. We'd managed to raise more than two million dollars.

"You know, we make a pretty good team." I smiled as we clinked champagne glasses. "I saw all of you working the crowd. Mira, how did you get McCloven to part with five hundred thousand dollars?"

She crossed her legs under her evening dress. "I told him that my friend Cassie was really impressed with the art collection in his apartment. She also mentioned that he was a fantastic dancer, and I told him we'd have to meet at one of Alex's clubs one night. Since Mrs. McCloven was headed our way, he pulled out his checkbook. Told me thank you, and that he'd appreciate it if I didn't mention his dabbling in art to anyone, especially his wife. It was a 'private thing'"—she made little quote marks in the air—"that he wanted to keep to himself. When she walked up, she wanted to know what we'd been discussing so thoughtfully. I sensed she was a little jealous. I said her husband was about to make a sizable donation of more than two hundred thousand dollars to the cause. You know how she is, always wanting to be the best, so she told him to double it. I thought he might drop dead right there on the spot."

"Mira, that's awful." I couldn't keep from laughing. "You blackmailed the poor man."

"That *poor man* is a multibillionaire who cheats on his wife with a different woman every week. He deserved a little karmic payback."

We all giggled. It felt good to release the tension of the last few days. "I have so much work to catch up on, but I'm going to sleep for a couple of hours first." I yawned.

"Hey, Gilly, I was curious about something," Alex chimed in. "You and Arath seem to be awfully comfortable with one another. In fact, you two made a beautiful couple on the dance floor."

"Leave it alone, Alex. We are not a couple. He came for business. I told you."

"Yeah. And he put on a tux and danced with you because…"

"We were at a ball." I knew what she was getting at, but I refused to go there. "Aren't you guys as curious as I am to know what Aunt Juliet said to him? And everything happened so fast, I didn't even get to talk to him about being a male mage."

Claire nodded. "I kind of wanted to talk to him, too. He has to know what he is. It's crazy that he's the ruler of a world full of demons and he isn't really one. Well, I guess technically he is, but there's not much demon in that DNA."

"Maybe, Gilly, you should—"

My cell phone interrupted Mira.

"Ms. Caruthers?" Jake was on the other end. "There's a problem."

"Demons?"

"It's Bailey. He's missing. We checked his flight and he never made it on the plane from Houston."

"Jake, you know how he is when he's down there. He's probably partying with his NASA buddies. He may not be home for a week."

"Yes, ma'am. I know. It's just he's off the grid. We aren't seeing him on the GPS. I'm afraid it's been disabled."

I sat up straighter and put my phone on speaker. "My sisters are here. Jake says Bailey is missing and he's off the grid." I felt guilty for not contacting the security team earlier when Claire couldn't find him. Tears welled in my eyes, but I refused to let them go. I was the strong one, and I wouldn't fall apart in front of my sisters.

While I spoke, I could tell Mira was trying to mentally connect with Bailey. When I saw a tear running down her cheek it was almost my undoing.

"I can't see him. I don't think he's in our world." She clasped her hands together.

I chewed on my lip. *Crap.*

"Okay, Jake. We may be looking at something otherworldly here. Or it may be related to"—it hurt to say the words—"to the murders. Georgia told me tonight that she felt like someone was watching her. Right now, we'll go on the assumption that someone may have taken him. He's worth a lot and they'll know it. They'll probably want some kind of ransom." I looked out the window to see where we were. "We'll be home in five minutes. Keep trying to track him, and you better contact Mom." I would have done it, but I didn't know where in the hell she was. I hung up the phone.

"Whoever took him is going to die. You know that, don't you?" Alex said. She may be an interior designer, and the ultimate party girl, but she protected our world from the dragons. She was born as tough as they come, and she had had a much easier time learning to kill than the rest of us.

"Amen to that," the soft-spoken Claire added. She had pulled her knees up to her chin, her pink toenails sneaking out under the hem of her dress.

Bailey and Claire were only ten months apart and they had an incredible bond. He was close to all of us, but those two were almost like twins. They had their own special language. Claire was always in trouble. Her curiosity about the world kept her on my mom's bad kid list. Whenever possible, Bailey took the blame. He could do no wrong in our mother's eyes, and he knew that from a very young age.

"All right. We need a plan. Alex, you call Kyle. I just talked to him about Georgia—tell him to make sure she's covered and to meet us at the house."

Claire stared at me. "Gilly, have you had one of your dreams lately?"

I shook my head. "Not in the last forty-eight hours or so. At least not a scary dream, anyway."

They all looked at me.

"It was a sexy dream, not really appropriate to share."

Their eyebrows went up, but no one said anything.

"I don't think he's dead," Mira finally said. "I would know. I mean, I can't connect with him, but he's a part of me, like you all are. If he no longer existed, I would know it."

Mira was the most sensitive of us, and she had a point. She always knew when we were hurt or if something was going on. She could read minds to a certain extent, but it gave her a migraine. So she usually relied on reading emotions.

If Mira was right and Bailey was still alive, we would find him.

CHAPTER

22

A half hour later, the four of us sat at the table in one of the large conference rooms of the security unit with Aunt Juliet, Mom, and Jake. Kyle was on the speakerphone.

Mom took the news better than I expected. She was always tough on the girls in the family. Dad had nurtured us and taught us about the arts and the world outside. He had helped each of us develop our public persona.

But it was our mother who had taught us hand-to-hand combat. She had also helped us to develop our powers and taught us how to use them. "The Guardian's life is a rewarding one, but she must always be prepared for the worst." That was Mom's motto.

But when it came to Bailey, all bets were off. He wasn't a

Guardian, though he had been educated as one. Everything we went through, he did. After sixteen years of martial arts training, he was capable of killing, though he'd never done it. Whoever took him must have had a battle on their hands. They had messed with the wrong family this time.

Aunt Juliet looked mad. "It's those damn dragons," she bit out between clenched teeth. "Hardheaded beasts. You saw what happened on their planet. They're doing this because they think we should have done something before their world was almost destroyed."

I looked over at Alex, and she folded her arms on the table. She hated the dragons as much as Juliet did, but something had happened to change the way she felt about the warrior Ginjin.

"I would agree with you, except we haven't had any jumpers," came Alex's careful reply. "Since we closed the portals the other day, only Ginjin has come through, and we know he didn't do it." Alex sat back in her chair. "But that doesn't mean they didn't pay someone else to do it. I don't trust them any more than you do."

We didn't have time to play the blame game. "Let's just stick with what we know." I had a pad of paper and a pen in front of me. Making notes while I talked always helped me to think. "Whoever has him has at least a two-hour jump, maybe more, on us. Mom, can you guys try to locate him with magic?"

She turned her hard stare on me. "Don't you think I've already tried?" Her voice was steely cold. Determined. She wore a long gold caftan. The reason she'd missed the ball was to work with the high council. They were still trying to help the dragons.

Aunt Juliet reached over and took my hand. "She's just worried, dear, that's why she's acting like a bitch."

There was a slight gasp around the table. No one ever disrespected my mother—except for Aunt Juliet. The petite blonde woman was never afraid to speak her mind. I had a feeling she was also angry with my mother about what had happened with Arath and Throe. I didn't blame her.

My mother's frown increased and I looked down at the table. There weren't many people or creatures who intimidated me, but my mother never failed in that respect. I'd stopped trying to win her favor years ago. I knew she loved us. She'd proven it a hundred times over in the way she cared for all of us. But she still scared the hell out of me.

"Sorry, Mom. I'm having a hard time with this. I mean, it's Bailey."

Her expression softened. "We're all tense, Gillian." She turned to Jake. "Did you find out anything from his friends in Houston?"

Jake jumped up and popped a DVD into the player and the screen on the wall lit up. "The hotel where he stayed sent us this copy of the security tape. It looks like he was abducted, but they were cool about it." We saw two men holding my brother up, as if he were drunk. I remembered what Kyle had said about the drug the ME hadn't been able to trace. Had they used it on Bailey?

His head was down, lolling from side to side, but there was no mistaking it was Bailey. His abductors' heads were down, too, and both men were bald. As they passed under the camera I saw something.

"Stop the video." I stood and walked closer to the large screen. "Back it up two frames."

Jake used the remote to do what I asked.

On the back of their necks there was a tattoo with symbols. A demon language that I recognized.

My jaw tightened and a growl escaped. Arath had some explaining to do.

"Jake, call the damn demon king and tell him I want a meeting."

"Your henchmen took my brother." I hadn't bothered with niceties. As soon as he passed through the portal, wearing his Levi's and a cotton shirt, I launched into a verbal attack. "Your demon brethren kidnapped him and have done God knows what. I want to know why you would let something like that happen. Since the portals are closed, how were they able to make it here without your knowledge? I mean, you told me yourself that you know who leaves and arrives on your world at any given time."

We were in the weapons room, and, lucky for him, everything was locked up. Arath had shut down the portal that Mond, the demon he thought might be an assassin, had used earlier. Arath had traveled through the Vex to meet me, but I was far from grateful that he'd risked his life to get there.

"You are still in your formal wear."

What the hell? "Brilliant observation, Arath. What the hell did you do to my brother?"

"I do not understand. Your brother is not in my world. Except for Mond, who used the dark magic, no one has passed through a portal on Maunra since we locked them." It bothered me that he didn't seem flustered at all.

"I saw the tattoos on the neck of the two men who kidnapped my brother. It was a demonic language, so cut the crap and tell me where he is."

His jaw jutted out slightly and his eyes glowed orange. "My word is my honor. If I tell you he is not on Maunra, then he is not." The last words were said menacingly.

"Look." I pulled out a picture we'd printed from the DVD of the kidnappers. "There." I pointed to the tats.

His eyes flashed orange.

As he reached out, the picture flew out of my hand and into his. Scary orange eyes, moved things with his mind, and glowed when he was angry. The list of Arath's powers seemed to grow each time we met.

"These are Amols. The slaves of the Manteros." He frowned at the picture. "They are evil, and while they may look demon, they are not from my world."

"How can you possibly know that? I know that language on

the tattoos. I've seen it used in writings from your world." My hands were on my hips. "What the hell is a Mantero?"

His left eyebrow rose. "The Manteros are most likely aligned with the darkness we've been fighting."

"So, what, it's like some secret society or something?"

"In a way, yes." He didn't elucidate.

"I'm sorry, am I missing something?"

"If these beings are involved, then you can expect things to get much worse."

"Lovely. Can I ask how you know that they didn't come from your planet?"

"I am aware of everything that passes through the portals in and out of my world."

"So you said before. Do you have some kind of tracking system?"

"Not in the way you think. I *know* these things. I feel them."

"That isn't possible." I shook my head. Who did this guy think he was?

He sighed. "You understand that I owe you no explanation."

I'd reached the end of my pleasant quotient for the night. "Arath, if your brother were missing, what would you do?"

Leaning back against the steel wall, he eyed me warily. "I've attuned my senses so that I'm aware of what passes through the portals to my world. I can feel when someone is there who shouldn't be, and when trouble is brewing. I don't always know who it is that wishes my world harm, but I sense it. No one arrives there unnoticed. I can track, as you say, at will. I tell you that your brother is not in my world.

"The markings on the necks of the Amols do suggest that someone from my world is involved in your brother's disappearance. They do work with the Manteros, but it has been many years since I've seen evidence of such. Most of the Amols have moved on to other worlds, but we have a few left. I will question them. If they have any knowledge of the situation I will take the information and then kill them for you."

"Thank you, but I would like to be there when you question them."

"That is not possible."

I had to make myself stop grinding my teeth. "Just take me to the Manteros. I will question them."

"Do you understand that I could kill you where you stand with a simple flick of my finger?" His voice was low and angry.

I looked at him. The glow had begun around him. I didn't care. Bailey's life was at stake and I didn't feel like wasting time arguing with a damn demon king.

"I did not intend to undermine your authority, King Arath. I'm certain if your brother were in peril you would want to question anyone who might know what was going on." My measured tone was meant to be reassuring and respectful, but I could tell he didn't take it that way from the way the muscles in his cheek ticked.

I wondered if the anger had more to do with my keeping

mum about his mother, than me showing disrespect. I wasn't proud of my actions, but I also didn't live life with regrets. I'd made some bad choices, but in the end it had worked out. Though it probably wasn't the time to tell Arath that.

"I will return through the Vex. If I discover information I will send it to you. There is no reason for you to waste time there when you should be searching elsewhere for your brother. If the Manteros are involved, and they seem to be, that means time is of the essence. Their prey seldom—" He stopped himself.

"What?"

"Make it out alive. Wherever they have taken your brother, he is in grave danger. The Manteros will take whatever it is they want from him and then kill him." The words were said in a matter-of-fact tone, but they hit me like boulders in a landslide.

I pressed the heel of my hand against my forehead. I could feel an ache beginning at my temple. In a few minutes the pain would surround my brain.

"There is an uprising on Maunra. I won't be able to keep all of the portals closed much longer, as I will need my power to stay alive. My people are upset about not being able to trade with other worlds. I will do my best to keep the Earth world safe, but I can make no promises." He turned his head toward the portal door as if he were listening to something. "I must go quickly. Trouble comes, and my world is in danger."

I sighed. "You must do what is necessary. I understand. But

I want you to know that I'm sorry I didn't tell you about your mother. It never seemed like the right time."

He turned his back to me. "You did what you thought was best. The dark magic isn't affecting just us; it is everywhere. I don't think any of us is going to be safe for much longer. Stay well, Guardian. Our universe depends on you."

"I—thank you." I said the last few words to air, as Arath had already passed through. It dawned on me that he'd come here even though he was under attack.

Then I had to go and be so rude.

"Sometimes, Gilly, you can be a real bitch."

CHAPTER

23

My headache had turned into a full-blown migraine by the time I made it to the kitchen. Kyle, who was dressed in jeans and his trademark black T-shirt, stood at the counter talking with Claire. The only time I'd seen him wear something different was when he'd donned a brown suit for my father's funeral. I only remembered because none of us had ever seen him in a tie.

He wore a Yankees ball cap over his buzz cut. The caps changed—in fact, I'd never seen him wear the same one twice. He had to have hundreds of them.

"Where is everyone?" I grabbed some of the herbs Mira kept on hand for headaches and put them in a loose bag to make a tea.

"There's been another shift. Many of the portals we closed are open again," Claire informed me. "Mom and the rest are doing their best to protect against the dark magic. The council is involved, which means at least everyone is paying attention."

The pain in my head became a tight band around my brain. Open portals meant eventually there would be jumpers. That's probably why Arath had had to leave so fast. "Any more word about Bailey?"

"I'm getting ready to fly down to Houston to see what I can find." Kyle sat on one of the barstools, leaning over a cup of coffee. His eyes were red and it looked as though he hadn't had much sleep. We'd soon be able to start our own insomniacs club.

"Kyle, do you think the murders might be connected with Bailey?"

He shrugged. "You know I don't really understand what's going on with all this otherworldly stuff, but I don't think it's coincidence. Someone wants something from you. I mean you specifically, Gillian. The murders were people that were associated with you. Maybe not best friends, but they were involved with you in some way. I can't find any other connection."

I pulled my hot cup from the microwave and took a sip even though I knew it would scald my tongue. "I've been thinking the same thing, but I don't know why. As far as I know, Markie and Reuben never even met. And I think someone was after Georgia— Wait, if you're here, where is she?"

"I had Jake send over two of his men to watch her. They'll make sure she gets to work in the morning."

"Good." I pulled myself up onto the kitchen counter forgetting I still wore my rather slippery silver dress. I almost slid off the edge before I caught my balance.

Claire smiled. "Hey, klutz, maybe you should take two minutes to change clothes." While I'd been talking to Arath, she'd put on her jeans and a "Save the Blue Whales" T-shirt.

"I will, I just need to get rid of this headache." I chewed on my lip. "Let's take a minute and work this out. It'd be easier if someone would remove the butcher knife from between my eyes." I circled my neck to ease the tension. "Kyle's right. There's some kind of connection. Markie was in real estate. She was helping me look for a gallery space in New York, and she'd found something in the SoHo area.

"Reuben was my number one guy for all things technical. He set up all the networks here, and—oh, crap. Claire, go get Jake."

I must have had a strange look on my face because she didn't even ask why.

"What is it?" Kyle pushed the barstool away. "Did you figure out a connection?"

"No, not really, but I need to ask Jake something. All the trouble with the portals began after Reuben's death."

Jake ran into the kitchen and almost ran into Kyle as he slid to a stop. "Did you find your brother?"

I set my cup down on the counter. "No. How often do you check for viruses in the system?"

Jake frowned. "I think it's something like every fifteen minutes. Why?"

"When the jumpers started going crazy, did you notice any blips in the system?"

He shook his head. "Not as far as I know, but I can run a report to see. What are you thinking?"

"Kyle mentioned that whoever was involved seems to have wanted something from me specifically. Markie and Reuben did have a meeting together to talk about what we needed for the tech aspects of the loft space for the gallery."

"Okay, there's nothing irregular about that." Claire had grabbed a pen and paper and was taking notes as I went along. "You guys do that for every gallery. And Reuben is—sorry, *was*—involved in almost all of our projects in some way or another—" She realized the same thing I did. "Gilly, do you think Reuben was a spy?"

I nodded. "I don't want to think that any more than you do. He'd been with us for years, and my God he was brilliant. Like you said, though, he was involved with all of us. He knew our every move. What projects were coming up, when we had problems with the portals. He and Bailey—"

"Worked together all the time," finished Jake. "You are on to something. So it's information. But why kill your friend Markie? And if they had such a great insider, why kill Reuben?"

"I think Markie saw something. When she came in early

for our meeting she met with Reuben first. Maybe she saw someone leave. I don't know, I'm just brainstorming here.

"As for Reuben, I don't know either. Maybe he had finished whatever it was they needed. Ya know what? Whoever it was, I bet a bag of diamonds Georgia saw them, too. Markie met with Reuben in my office because the conference room was busy."

"I better send over some more men to your assistant's house." Jake had already pulled out his cell. "I think we should bring her back here. If Reuben was compromised, we may have bugs in the system. We'll run a full diagnostic, and we'll also comb his place for more information. The police didn't find any incriminating evidence, but then they didn't know about all of this."

"You've got your hands full, I'll take care of the house." Kyle pulled his car keys out of his pocket. "I've got a friend in Houston I can call to cover our bases down there. He'll check with the NASA friends, and he's good with the CSI crap. If there's anything in that hotel room, he'll find it."

I took a deep breath. "We're going to find him."

Claire squeezed my hands in hers. "Damn right. Now go change your clothes, we have work to do."

By the time I'd changed, Jake had a report ready for me in the control room. "We've got a real mess on our hands. There's a virus set to go off like a time bomb in our tracking system. We don't know how long we have to figure out the problem, and once it goes off my techies think it will conceal all of the jumpers. We won't know who or what is coming over or from where."

"What about the backup system?"

He shook his head. "There is no backup system now. It's been wiped clean by some kind of internal coding."

Okay. "Well, then we're going to have to do things the old-fashioned way." Guardians had been protecting Earth for thousands of years, since long before computers were ever invented. We had an extra sense that all of us could tap into. It took a great deal of energy, but we could use it to track if necessary. "Alert Mom and my sisters. And do whatever it takes to get that system back online. Reuben was as smart as they come, but there are great people on the team at Caruthers Corp.—someone should be able to destroy this virus."

Bailey could do it, which was probably one of the many reasons why he was missing. Whoever had him had to know they had a gold mine with that brain. That would work to our advantage because there was a really good chance they would try to use my brother to get to us, which meant he would stay alive. "I need a few minutes to think. Let me know if anything happens." Mira's miracle medicine hadn't worked as fast as I would have liked. I made myself calm down. Stress only made things worse and I needed all my brain cells to find my brother.

Jake went into his glassed-in office just off of the control room. I headed back to my bedroom. It was peaceful there.

I knew I should be doing something to help close the portals again, but I felt that I was on to something. Just at the edge of my brain was a thought that would not come to fruition.

"Be logical." I sat at the desk facing my window. The sun peeked over the tree-covered hills. I focused on the view and let my mind wander. The demons had to be working for someone. Arath said they usually dealt with Fae, so I needed to talk to Mira about that. She would have a better idea of who would do something like this.

I wasn't sure why, but I trusted Arath enough to believe him when he said his people weren't involved. I couldn't keep my thoughts from straying to our dancing earlier in the evening. Our bodies had fit perfectly together, and when he touched me...

Oh, my God, Gill. Get it together. You're lusting after a half demon, half mage, and your brother's been kidnapped. Not to mention the world may be ending.

I leaned my chin on my hands and rubbed my temples. Thanks to Mira's herbs the pain in my brain was a dull ache now.

Staring down at the paper, I tried to connect the dots. Markie had obviously stumbled on to something. There was no other explanation. Reuben wasn't the kind of guy she'd date, so it was tied to business. I just couldn't figure out how.

And Reuben. It broke my heart that he'd betrayed our family. We'd trusted him with our most precious secrets, and he and Bailey had been friends for years—since long before he ever came to work for us. None of this made any sense.

Someone knocked on the door and it made me jump. I laughed at my nervousness.

"Yes?"

"It's me—Jake."

"Come in." I turned to face the door.

"This was left with the gate guard two minutes ago. He said it came by a courier, and we're checking out the driver and the company." He handed me latex gloves and I noticed he had on a pair, too. "Just in case we can pick up some prints besides the guard's."

Once I'd donned the gloves, he handed me a letter opener. "We scanned it to make sure there are no toxins involved."

His words made me hold the thing by the corners as he handed it to me. Leave it to Jake to think of everything. He put down a piece of plastic on my desk and I slid the opener across the cream-colored envelope. The heavy paper made me think of an invitation to a party, of which we received hundreds each month. Of course, invitations seldom came by special courier at six in the morning.

There was a single sheet of paper inside with one sentence typed in bold letters.

Kill the demon king, or your brother dies.

CHAPTER

24

Demons, prepared for battle, crowded the great hall. The rooms were packed with beasts of every imaginable size and form. Some floated, others walked on two or four legs. Two huge troll-looking things had to duck down to fit inside the two-story foyer.

No one paid attention to me. I slipped through the great hall and found Arath's second in command, Clede.

"I must see the king." I gave him my most authoritative stare.

"He does not wish to be disturbed." Clede waved one of his paws toward the crowd. "We prepare for battle."

"I can see that. It—it won't take long, but it's imperative I see him right now. The state of the universe depends on it."

Oh, the lies. "He'll be angry with you if you don't do as I ask. I promise you this is of the utmost importance."

The grumpy demon gave me a weird look, almost if he were appraising me in some way. It sent a chill down my spine. "I have news from the council. He must hear what I have to say before he goes into battle."

It became more difficult by the second to keep a straight face.

He didn't say anything for at least a minute, just continued to give me that weird stare. Then he turned and motioned for me to follow him.

We went through several long hallways, and finally he pounded on a door.

"Yes?"

"The Guardian wishes to speak with you, my lord," Clede hissed through his fangs.

The door opened.

The demon king's armor, which consisted of an intricate carved silver breastplate and leather pants, made him look even more magnificent. Weapons were stashed in a leather belt around his waist and a sword hung at his shoulder. The sight of him took my breath away.

He watched as I entered the room. The look in his eyes held something I couldn't decipher.

Is he sorry I'm here? God, why does he have to be so handsome? I can't do this.

"I—well. You're obviously going into battle." I blabbered

the words, nervous. "It's inconsiderate of me to even be here. Did you find out anything about Bailey?" The words tumbled out of my mouth at an alarming rate. I'd never been so nervous.

"Is that why you are here, for information about your brother?" He turned his back to me. With his neck unprotected I had the perfect opportunity to slice his head from his body. There was one big problem. I couldn't seem to get my hand or my sword to cooperate. The weapon sat in the harness at my back, and my hand stayed by my side. I cared too much for him. As much as he frustrated me, he was a good man.

So was my brother.

Kill him. My mind ordered. "Why are you going into battle?" *That wasn't what I meant to say.*

"It is not your concern."

"Why do you do that?"

He turned. "What is that?"

"You argue every point. I could have asked any demon in the great hall who they were gathered to fight, and they would have told me."

"Then perhaps you should do so. As you can see, I am busy."

The man was nothing short of infuriating. "You didn't answer my question. Do you have any news about Bailey?"

His right fist tightened and I could see that it took effort to make it relax. "I have more important matters to deal with than a Guardian's missing brother." Arath continued to stare at me. I finally recognized the look. Disappointment. For some reason that bothered me more than anger ever could.

"What did I do?" I had to know.

"It's what you came here to do." His voice was so soft it barely registered and I wondered if he had really said the words, or if I'd only imagined it. "Tell me, Guardian. Why are you here?"

I closed my eyes and took a deep breath. "I came to speak with you about something. It can wait."

"You came with a purpose; will you leave without fulfilling it?" His hand at his side clenched again, betraying his anger.

"I don't know what you are talking about." I gave him my best lawyer stare. I'd spent years perfecting that poker face.

"The note in your back pocket says otherwise."

He couldn't know about that. Jake had made a copy for me before I left, and I was in such a hurry, I hadn't even remembered slipping it into my back pocket.

"You must kill me or your brother dies. You were going to mate with me, and then slit my throat. I expected more from you than a cowardly killing. I deserve more."

I sank back against the door. There was no use in arguing. "How did you know?"

"Where you are concerned, Guardian, I know everything." He didn't call me Gillian anymore and small part of my heart died. I really cared for him, and it mattered to me what he thought about me.

When the hell did that happen?

"You read my mind." The statement hung in the air like an accusation, but I was most definitely the guilty party. "Then you know I couldn't go through with it."

"Still you came." The words hung in the air.

A knock on the door made me jump.

"Your Highness, we must go." It was Clede. "Their forces crest the mountain."

"A moment," Arath called back. "You must go, Guardian. It is not safe for you here. There's a good chance I will die in battle today and then you will have your brother back. Will that make you happy?"

He could have punched me in the stomach and it wouldn't have hurt any less.

I shook my head, unable to speak. A tear slid down my cheek. "You won't die by my hand or anyone else's today." The words came out in a sob. "I'm sorry, but you aren't going to die until I've had a chance to make you understand. I did come here with murder on my mind, but I couldn't do it. Don't you understand? I care about you."

"Guardians don't cry." Arath bent to pull his pant leg over his boot, but I saw the careful look he gave me before he bent down.

When he stood up, I reached out a hand and touched the silver breastplate. "I want to hate you enough to kill you and save my brother but I can't. What kind of magic have you used on me, Arath?"

"It is you who wields the power, Guardian. I fear you have

weakened me. I should kill you where you stand, but all I want to do is this."

His kiss sent fire through my body and made me tremble. When he backed away, I almost cried from the loss of him.

There were shouts in the hallway. Armor clanked and the troops were ready.

"I do not have time for this. *Gorstat*," he barked, and a portal opened up at the word. "Go." The words came out in a growl.

"Arath, please know I couldn't have gone through with it. I would never cause you harm. I only wanted your help," I whispered as I moved toward the portal. "No matter what happens to either of us, know that I care for you."

As I reached the entrance I turned back to look at him. A glorious sight in his armor, his eyes glowed and his muscles rippled with sheer power. "Do not return." He growled again. "It is no longer safe for your kind on Maunra."

The energy of the portal pulled me through and I landed in our control room seconds later.

Mira waited for me with her eyes closed as if she were sensing something. "I knew you couldn't do it." She sighed. "Thank God. You would have never been able to live with yourself."

"He's a damn demon: of course I could have done it. I'm a Guardian. I do what's necessary." My heart tore into tiny bits as I put my weapons away. Tears threatened to fall.

She snorted. "Gilly, don't go there. You know you care for him, and he's a powerful mage, not just a demon. And I think it's possible you are in severe like with him." She held up a hand to stop my protests. "There's no sense arguing about it. You don't cry, so the tears speak volumes. Killing him would not have brought Bailey back. Whoever is doing this only wanted Arath out of the way."

"You can't know that." I pinched the bridge of my nose to keep from crying more. So much had happened in the last few days that I hadn't even stopped to examine my feelings. Mira was right. I did care for the demon king. "God, I can't tell the rest of them that I didn't get the job done."

"Your family will be relieved you didn't kill the one man you've really cared about in the last five years," Alex said as she entered the room, Claire on her heels.

"He's not a man. He's a demon," I snarled at them. *God, why do they all have to be so damn intuitive?*

"Um, yeah, about that." Claire stepped up and took my hand. "When he's with you, I get a very human vibe from him. We saw you at the ball. He cares for you, Gilly."

That was something I couldn't think about. The idea that he might care for me as much as I did him made what I'd just done unforgivable.

I shook my head, trying to wipe away the thoughts. *Heart, you can break later.*

"Are you all insane? We don't have time for this foolishness. Our brother is missing. And I'm going to get him back."

I tried not to notice their pitying glances as I pushed through the three of them.

* * *

An hour later I paced back and forth in my room. Part of me tried to strategize and decide my next move to find my brother. The other half of me wondered if Arath was still alive. I thought about asking Mira, but I couldn't do it. It was silly to waste her power for my own whims.

Please, God, let him live. Even if I never get to see him again, I need him to survive today. I blew out a breath to keep the tears from falling. I didn't have time to cry.

My cell rang. *Saved by the bell.* Thankful for the distraction, I picked up the phone.

"Yes?"

"Hi, it's Georgia."

Poor girl. I'd totally forgotten about her. "How are you? Did Jake's men bring you here to the house?"

There was a long pause. "No, I had them bring me to the office. I did speak with Jake and he asked me to think if I'd seen anyone with Reuben. God, I still can't believe he's dead." She sniffled. "I didn't want to say anything, because I just feel so damn guilty."

"Georgia, what is it? Just tell me, maybe I can help."

"No. It's—you've been so good to me, and I promise you I had no idea what was going on. He told me he was trying to simplify the record keeping. That he needed to create a database so that you guys would have instant information about any world you might be dealing with, and that it would revolutionize the way you could access the system."

As she went on, my stomach tightened. "Georgia, tell me what you're talking about." I found it difficult to keep the nervous edge from my voice.

"I gave Reuben access to your father's files. The entire history of the Guardians."

I sat, well, more fell, back onto the side of my bed. "Why didn't you tell me?"

She sobbed again. "He told me he'd cleared it with you and that it was part of some kind of larger upgrade. You were gone last week when it all began, and...God, there's no excuse. I just assumed it was okay. I had no reason not to trust him. I mean, it was Reuben. I'm such an idiot."

Crap. There was no telling who he'd given that information to. I knew he hadn't been working on any updates. We'd just gone through a full revamp.

"Georgia, stop crying. Please. We all trusted him. It's not your fault. He's been working with us for years, and you had every right to believe him. Yes, I wish you'd checked with me." *Bailey might still be here if you had.* "But it's a mistake any of us could and did make. The man's totally jacked our system and no one suspected anything. Tell me the truth, please—did anything else happen? Did you see him with anyone?"

I could hear her take a steadying breath. "Jake asked the same thing. People come and go around here all the time. I can't remember. I promise, I'll sit down and try, but right now I can't think of anyone out of the ordinary."

"It's crazy for you to try to work today, and I'm worried about your safety. Whoever killed Markie and Reuben may be after you. We all feel certain you've seen the killer; you just haven't realized it yet. I want Jake's men to bring you out here to the house. You need some rest, and maybe once you sleep, you'll be able to remember something."

"I—feel like I should resign," Georgia said. "I screwed up big-time. I liked him. I mean, we even went out a couple of times and I'd stopped by his house to feed his cat when he was out of town. He was my friend."

"Trust, me, Georgia, he used us all. I know how betrayed you feel. And you aren't resigning. That's the last thing I need right now. Who the hell would run the company while I'm out saving the world?"

She gave a sad laugh. "I can't come out there right now, there's so much work here to do."

"Bring it with you. But I want you here where we can keep you under tight security."

"I'm never going to be able to say I'm sorry enough."

I grunted. "We all have regrets right now. Let's just move on. Gather all the paperwork together, and I'll make the arrangements for them to bring you here."

As I hung up, the phone rang again. "Yes?"

"Mademoiselle Caruthers?"

"Yes, Che." He was the manager of my Paris gallery.

"There is terrible news." His heavy French accent sounded worried.

Oh, God, what now?

"Che, whatever it is, it's going to have to wait. I have a family emergency."

"I apologize, I would not have called unless absolutely necessary, but this is very serious."

Che had always been so dedicated, but now was not the time to argue over something as trivial as what color to paint the front door. That had taken us two weeks to decide, and then we took several more days to settle on the perfect shade of blue. Every detail was of great importance to him. I had a feeling he wouldn't get off the phone unless I listened to what he had to say.

"Okay. Lay it on me."

He sobbed. "There has been a murder in the gallery."

CHAPTER

25

The Paris gallery was located in the Latin Quarter,
the cultural heart of the city. It was the first one I'd opened,
because I had felt if I could make it in Paris, I could replicate
it elsewhere. I'd been right.

While it was the smallest of all the galleries I owned, it was
also the most successful. All the lights were on and the police
had cordoned off the entrance. Curious pedestrians who tried
to peek in were shooed away by the uniformed officers. Thankfully, the reporters and photographers were behind barricades,
so I didn't have to deal with them immediately.

My driver let me off in the street, as there was no way to
pull in close to the entrance. After a few explanations to those
guarding the outside, I was allowed in.

"Mademoiselle Caruthers, I appreciate you coming so quickly." The officer, who was dressed in a black suit, white shirt, and blue tie, reached out a hand. "I am Inspector Claude."

I shook his hand. "I'm surprised you're still here. I received the call almost ten hours ago." I knew the police might be suspicious if I suddenly showed up a few minutes after Che called. Even though we can teleport, we have to be really careful about that sort of thing. It was also important for the paparazzi to catch us coming out of airports now and then. It still killed me to be stuck on a plane for nine hours when I should have been searching for Bailey. Thankfully, I had my sisters, who promised to keep me informed.

He nodded. "We wish to be very thorough in our investigation. It takes several hours to cover a crime scene such as this."

We stood in the open foyer, just inside the door. "He told me that it was Jona Lathers who was killed. Is that correct?"

"*Oui*. The artist was murdered here in the gallery, and the body moved to the backroom. Monsieur Che discovered the man when he came in this morning. There was no sign of forced entry, and your manager did not realize anything amiss until he went into the storage room to check on something."

The idea that the talented Jona was gone broke my heart. He was an amazing artist who could make a chalk painting look like a masterpiece. He was also a great friend to Che. I leaned against the reception desk. "Poor Che, is he still here? Has he been able to help you? I must admit it's been two months since I've even been here. We stay in contact through the phone and e-mail."

The officer shook his head. "*Non*. One of my people took him home to rest. He was quite distressed."

"I don't understand how this could happen. Do you have any idea who could have done it?"

"We know it was someone the artist knew, as he had let them in the front door. We have several leads, as you Americans say, but I have a few questions for you."

"Certainly." Even though I'd spent the last nine hours on the family's private jet, I was exhausted. I couldn't rest. Kyle and Jake had been keeping me updated on the situations with my brother and the computer hacking. All I really wanted to do was to crawl into a hole and disappear for a few hours. "You may ask me anything."

"Do you have anyone who would wish you harm?"

I shrugged. "My family is involved in several businesses, and it is difficult not to make enemies along the way if one is to be successful." We also guarded Earth from other beings, so there were people all over the universe who might wish us harm.

"Yes, I understand this. I'm asking if there is someone who might have been closer to you. This seems to have been a very personal crime."

He wanted something specific, but I couldn't figure out what it was.

"Inspector, I don't mean to be rude, but if there is something you'd like me to address, please tell me. It was a personal crime, but Jona suffered much more than me. So please just ask your question."

He motioned to one of the other police officers, who brought over a plastic evidence bag. I was careful not to let on, but I knew as soon as I saw the stationery inside. It matched the note I'd received earlier about Arath.

"This was found on the body." The inspector flipped over the bag so that I could read the note.

Gillian,
You disappointed me.
You are next.

It was in the same typewritten text as the last note.

"I ask again, do you have any idea who would write something like this?"

"No." It was an honest answer. *It could be anyone in the universe.* Of course, I couldn't say that to him.

"You do not seem as disturbed as I might have thought. Have you received something like this before?" The inspector was obviously good at his job, but so was I.

I put on my lawyer face. I couldn't tell him about the note telling me to kill the demon king, because demons didn't exist. "No." I had a feeling it was all tied in to Bailey, but I didn't have a clue why. "If you check with the Austin police in Texas, you'll see there have been two murders of people I knew. One was an employee, the other a friend." I wondered why I hadn't seen this murder in a dream as I had the others, but then it dawned on me that I hadn't actually been asleep in a couple of days.

I pulled out a card with Kyle's information. "This is a private investigator who works with my family." I wrote down Jake's number. "Our head of security may also be able to help you. He and Kyle have been working on this together. I know it is a great favor to ask, but would it be possible for you to fax a copy of the letter to them?"

"It is no problem at all. So do you think we have a transcontinental serial killer?"

"As I said before, I don't know. I'm not a detective, but the murders at home are definitely related. I'd rather not see photos, but was the body posed in a certain way? Were the bones broken so that the legs and arms were bent in an unnatural position? And did they cut out his heart?" I shivered when I said the words. I'd seen many gruesome things in my day, but these murders hit way too close to home. No matter how much Reuben had betrayed our family, he didn't deserve to die the way that he had. And Jona and Markie were just in the wrong place at the wrong time. I felt certain about that.

"Yes." The inspector stared at me. "I will talk to these detectives. Mademoiselle, I would appreciate it if you would stay in the city for at least the next forty-eight hours should we have any more questions."

That wouldn't be possible. I needed to get back to search for Bailey. There was also the problem of the new jumpers since there had been another universal shift. "I will try, but I'm afraid I have business back in the States that is very important. I'm not sure how much longer I can stay. I will, however, make sure I'm available by phone, and should you need me to return I will do so."

He gave me another long look. They had no reason to hold me here. This was one of those times when my lawyer skills came in very handy. If they tried to detain me, I had many friends in Paris and he knew it. Besides, I wasn't a suspect. In fact it very much looked like I might be the next victim.

Like I'd let that happen.

"You understand that your life is in danger?"

I didn't laugh but I wanted to. My life was always danger.

"I do. I want to visit Che, to make sure he is okay." Che was such a sensitive man, and I knew he'd been friends with the artist. "I also want to see if there is anything I can do for Jona's family, and of course we will take care of the arrangements to send his body home to the States."

The inspector nodded.

I handed him another card. "You may call me anytime."

"I would prefer while you are in the city that one of our officers travel with you. Your safety is important to us."

I'd also be a giant piece of bait to draw the killer out, and it would be handy to have an officer nearby to catch him or her. There was just one problem: I wasn't going to be around long enough to let that happen.

I smiled. "That is kind of you, but I know how shorthanded

you must be. My driver is a highly trained bodyguard. I will be fine." I certainly could hold my own against any foe, but I hadn't minded that Jake had sent Max with me. Not only was he the size of a bulldozer, he was a trained assassin in martial arts. I'd sparred with him several times, and walked away with more than a few bruises. The guy never held back, even when fighting with us girls.

"I hope you are correct. I'd like to ask you one last thing." He crossed his arms in front of his chest.

"Yes?"

"Is there any reason why the murderer would take all of the paintings done by the artist known as Emilio?"

I looked past him to the large white wall on the right. The three paintings that had been hanging there were gone.

Oh. My. God.

Che's apartment was just down from the Buci, a small boutique hotel near Saint-Sulpice.

I'd never seen him in anything other than a suit and tie, but he wore jeans and a sweater when he answered the door to his apartment.

His eyes were red-rimmed. From the pain etched on his face it looked as though he and Jona had become much more than friends. I'd hired Che straight out of college three years earlier. He had a better eye for art than most people who had been in the business much longer. I'd never even suspected his relationship with Jona. They had been more than discreet about it.

"Che, I'm sorry." I reached out my arms to hug him, and he wrapped his around me. "It must have been horrible for you to find Jona like that."

Sniffling, he pulled me from the entry. "I just opened a bottle of wine. Please share it with me."

I followed him into the tiny apartment, though by Paris standards it probably cost close to half a million. The furniture was an eclectic mix of antiques and more traditional pieces. Art lined every wall.

"I know I shouldn't be surprised, but you have an amazing collection."

Che pursed his lips as he poured the wine. "You are quite generous with my salary. My mother left me this place, so most of what I make goes to investments and art. Well"—he held up the bottle—"and great wine."

We sat on a soft gray sofa. He had a selection of cheeses and a few pieces of fruit on a china plate.

There was no delicate way to steer the conversation back to the matter at hand, so I decided to just go for it. "Do you know if Jona had family? I'd like to speak with them, and to make arrangements for his funeral."

Che sighed. "He was alone. A drunk driver killed his parents and sister several years ago. I know you don't like us to date the artists, but Jona and I had been going out long before you chose him to show in the gallery."

I leaned back. "You never said anything. You let me think I'd discovered him and then you became friends."

"You did discover him, in that café across from the gallery. I made sure the manager had a few pieces of Jonas's work on his walls. I knew if you saw it, you'd want him. He was—so talented." Che stared off into space for a moment, willing his tears away.

I patted his knee. "You could have just told me."

He shrugged. "Honestly, it was Jona who refused my help. He wanted so much to prove himself. He was excited about his upcoming show, and couldn't sleep last night. He left about three this morning to finish the installation of the new pieces." He sobbed. "I brought in coffee and croissants around nine, and when I didn't see him I tried to call. I heard his phone ringing in the backroom. I called to him, but he didn't answer."

As he remembered, Che crumbled. Tears stained his cheeks. "How could someone do that to him? There was not a kinder, more tender soul."

I disagreed. There was a reason Jona and Che were well matched. I took his hand in mine and squeezed. "I've said this so many times the last few days, but I don't know how someone could be so horrible. It's senseless and incredibly disturbing. The police think it may be related to some murders in the States."

Che didn't say anything.

I sighed. "I'm sure the police have asked you this a hundred different ways, but has anyone visited the gallery in the last few days? Maybe someone who seemed out of place or suspicious?"

He closed his eyes as if trying to recall. "Our usual clientele. No one I would suspect of murder. Emilio came looking for you. He was upset when he found out you weren't in town. Seems he had been trying to get in touch with you and someone told him that you'd be here. I asked if you'd had a spat, and he told me it was just a misunderstanding he needed to clear up with you. He asked if you had changed your numbers, and I told him no.

"He didn't seem happy that Mademoiselle Stewart had bought one of his paintings. He wanted to know the shipping date."

Emilio again. I'd slept with the guy and he was a creep, but a murderer? I didn't see his sensitive artist nature allowing him to do something like cutting out a heart. Or breaking bones to stage—I almost choked on my wine. Had he been creating still life?

No. It wasn't possible. A lothario most certainly, but surely I would have known if I'd been sleeping with a murderer.

I shivered again.

Che set down his glass of wine. "He's going to be very upset when he finds out his paintings have been stolen. I told him we had interest in both of the nudes. He seemed pleased about that, so I thought it strange that he didn't want the other painting to go to Mademoiselle Stewart."

Nothing about Emilio made sense, except that for some

reason he was in the middle of this big mess. For the life of me, I couldn't figure out how.

I talked with Che for a while longer, moving the subject to different things, hopefully taking his mind off his troubles.

Outside Che's apartment the paparazzi and reporters had gathered, the lights from the flashes temporarily blinding me.

"Ms. Caruthers, can you comment on zee murder at zee gallery?" I couldn't see who asked the question. The lights burned my eyes and everything was a blur. I couldn't even see the faces of those who surrounded me less than a foot away.

"No." I held up a hand over my eyes to see if I could see the car. There were at least twenty photogs and reporters between the street and me.

I sighed. "Please, I'd like to get through." As I stepped forward they closed in. I'd called for the car but I doubted my driver/bodyguard, Max, could see me in the crowd.

"Are you responsible for the death of—"

"That's enough," a man bellowed. I caught a glance of a huge figure cutting through the melee. "She is in mourning for her friend. This is no time to harass someone in mourning." Max grabbed my arm roughly and pulled me through the crowd, shoving the reporters out of the way.

The car door was open and I climbed in. Max slammed the door behind me. Before I could get situated, he'd pulled away from the curb. "I'm sorry, Ms. Caruthers. When you called I was a few blocks down, only place I could park on these narrow streets."

"Max, don't worry about it. I should have known they'd catch up with me eventually. I'm just grateful you were here."

"Jake wouldn't have it any other way. We're all on high alert and we know the family is in danger. I won't be so far away the next time."

The universe is in danger. "Well, I for one am happy to have someone like you around right now. How long till we hit Orly?"

"Traffic's bad, probably an hour."

"Thanks." I picked up the cell and dialed Kyle's number. I had a job for him.

"We need to find Emilio," I said as soon as he answered.

"What? The ex?"

"I think he knows our killer. Hell, he may be the killer. He's definitely involved somehow and I'm going to kick his ass when I see him."

Kyle gave a slight chuckle.

"What?" Anger tinged my tone. Just thinking about the jerk had my nerves on edge.

"I'm really glad my name isn't Emilio." Kyle clicked off the phone.

CHAPTER

26

My breath made tiny clouds. I'd been running, and my lungs ached. Someone had been chasing me, but when I turned to look behind me, darkness followed.

It took me a minute to realize I was in the middle of a dream. The weird thing was, I couldn't remember the first part of it, but I'd most definitely been running.

"Where am I?" One of the things I'd been able to do when the dreams began was to control my own thoughts and actions. I'd learned as a child to be an observer, especially during nightmares, so that I wasn't so frightened by the scary images that sometimes plagued me.

This was different.

I had no control. I tried to visualize my bedroom at home.

When that didn't work I thought about my sisters and their laughter.

A chill settled over me, as all I saw was the darkness. No buildings or people, but something heavy and evil was near.

Get out, Gilly.

"Hello, Slayer." The voice sent an eerie chill down my spine that had nothing to do with the frigid air.

"Who are you?" Still there was nothing but inky blackness around me. My feet were on the ground, but now it was difficult to move my arms and legs. Someone had a hold on me. The thing had trapped me.

"I've been watching you," the creepy voice finally answered.

In my line of work I deal with the creepy and gross all the time, but this thing was the darkest evil I'd ever come across. Something in me wanted to give over to it, to just let it consume me.

No. You never give in. Fight. "That's great. Why don't you come out where I can see you?" My voice shook a tiny bit, but didn't betray how I really felt inside. "Why won't you tell me who you are?"

"Think about it, Slayer. You know who I am. You've always known."

"Uh, no. I'm asking you simple questions even an idiot could understand, and you're trying to get all metaphysical on me."

"Insolent witch!" the voice roared. It had a faint accent with a European sound, perhaps a being from another planet that had learned English from tapes or books. And the hollowness of it was almost as if a spirit spoke through another person. I'd seen someone possessed many years ago, and I remembered that dead sort of voice.

"Hey, I'm not the one interrupting a good night's rest. Last thing I remember is staring at my thirtieth cup of coffee in two days. Then I wound up here. The way I see it, it's my dream and I can offend you if I want."

A growl emanated from the darkness and a hand tightened around my throat. "You did not do as I wished, so you are going to die with the knowledge that your brother will soon follow."

Bailey. This monster had my brother. "Where is he? If you're so all-powerful, why won't you let me see him?"

The voice laughed, but it wasn't a pleasant sound. "His current state might disturb you, Slayer. I will save you that one horror before you die." The hand tightened more and breathing became difficult.

My fighting instincts kicked in, but it was useless since my arms and legs were paralyzed. There was also the problem of me not being able to see my opponent.

My dream, I take control. I couldn't fight physically, so I'd do it mentally.

I tried to force myself to wake up but it didn't work.

"You are powerless, Guardian. Stop fighting. Unless you want to die slowly."

Death? People don't die from dreams. The hand around my neck squeezed tight. *Okay, maybe they do.*

I coughed and my chest ached from lack of air. I tried to talk but it was impossible. I refused to let this monster get the best of me.

A strange noise, shouting. *What is that?*

Something wet hit my face. I coughed and the screaming grew louder. The thing pushed against my face, and then shook my shoulders. Contact. I reached out for whatever it was and this time it worked.

I woke to find Max standing over me screaming, "Ms. Caruthers, I insist you wake up now. Or I'm going to slap you."

I laughed, only slightly hysterically. "Max, you precious man. I think you just saved my life." I gave his arm a squeeze, grateful for the reality of it. Even though my body still shivered from the cold, I shoved the cashmere blanket off me. "I'm not sure, but I think the killer just tried to murder me in my dreams. He would have succeeded if it hadn't been for you."

"You were making strange noises and it sounded like you were choking." Max handed me a towel to wipe away the water he'd splashed on me. "I'm sorry about your clothes. I tried to wake you by talking, but you didn't budge. I thought you were about to choke to death."

"I was. Whatever it was had its hands around my neck. I've had a lot of nightmares but none as scary as that one. Yikes. I need to drink some more coffee. I'll be damned if I'm going to fall asleep again."

I picked up the phone and called Kyle and Jake. We had to

catch whoever or whatever this thing was and we had to do it fast. Otherwise I would never be able to sleep again.

Hours later we landed, and I was grateful to see no paparazzi at the airport. Max had the car on the road in a matter of minutes, and I leaned my head back against the headrest.

"Max, let's stop by Taco Bell on the way home. I'm in serious need of a grilled steak–stuffed burrito."

Half grunting, half laughing, he turned his head back. "Yes, ma'am."

Five minutes later we pulled into the drive-through. "Would you like me to take care of it?"

"Nah, go ahead and pull up. I'll order. What would you like?"

"I'll take a half-pound cheesy bean burrito and a Gordita Baja. Oh, and a large Slice, if you don't mind."

I couldn't help but smile. Max was a man after my own heart. After placing the order at the kiosk, he pulled the car up so I could get the food.

"That's seventeen sixty-two." The girl with the headset and six earrings on her right ear smiled. Her bleached-blonde hair was in a ponytail and she wore bright pink lipstick. "Oh. My. God. You're totally Gillian Caruthers." She jumped up and down. "I just saw you in *OK* with that hot dude—oh, sorry.

Um." The caption below the picture must have dawned on her: "Gillian Caruthers's dumpee #25. When will she find Mr. Right?"

I handed her the money. "It's okay. Guys suck, right?"

"Hell, yeah." She clapped her hand over her mouth. "Sorry, we're not supposed to cuss at work. Can I ask you, like, a huge favor?"

"Depends. What is it?" I took the plastic bags and the drinks from her and handed Max his portion of the bounty.

"Could I get a picture with you? I know, it's superlate, and you probably want to get home. But I think you're the coolest. I mean, you're a lawyer and you run a company. Then you always land these hot guys, and the clothes—don't even get me started. You're, like, a huge inspiration. I'm only a senior in high school, but I'm going to study law when I get to college. I want to be just like you."

I bet her parents weren't happy about that. Most of the world thought I was a spoiled, rich bitch whose daddy paid to get me through law school. Laughing, I looked behind us and saw there was no one in line. "Do you have a camera?"

"No, but I have my phone." She pulled it out of her pocket.

"Max, can you pull up a little so I can get out? What did you say your name is?"

"Caitlan Langton, and you are just the best."

I was a bit crumpled and I had no doubt this picture would

be all over the Internet in a matter of seconds, but I couldn't disappoint her.

"How about we let my friend here take the picture?" I took the phone from her and handed it to Max. He fiddled with the buttons for a moment. "Smile," he said.

Caitlan leaned through the window and I did my best to put my arm around her shoulder. She beamed, and so did I.

"My friends aren't going to believe this." She was still smiling as Max gave her her phone back. "I knew you were nice. I've seen some of the things they've been saying. I promise I'll get the word out that you're totally cool."

My own teen PR agent. "I appreciate it." I reached out a hand. "Caitlan, you are one rockin' chick." I reached into my purse and handed her a card. "This has my private e-mail. It's just for you. I want you to e-mail me and let me know how school is going."

She held the card to her heart. "I promise to never show anyone. It means so much that you shared it with me. Oh, my gosh, I might cry."

I laughed again. "Don't you dare. I'm kind of tired and if you start I will, and then I'll be really embarrassed. We've got to run, but you keep in touch, okay?"

"I will. Thank you!" she yelled just before Max slammed the door closed.

"That was a nice thing you did," he said as he pulled back on the highway. "That's something she's going to remember the rest of her life."

"What she doesn't know is it's something I won't forget anytime soon. She was a sweet kid." I'd make sure she didn't have to worry about paying for law school.

I took out my burrito and took a bite. Closing my eyes, I savored the spicy beef. *Now this is worth saving the universe.*

CHAPTER

27

Back at home I discovered Kyle and Jake had run out of leads. I'd learned more on my short sojourn to Paris and in my wickedly bad nightmare than everyone else combined.

Jittery with nerves, I almost took Jake's head off when he told me that they had hit a dead end. Hands shaking, I grabbed the edge of the kitchen counter, which held my fortieth cup of coffee in two days, and willed myself to get Zen.

I took a deep breath. "Well, now you know that Emilio wasn't happy about Markie buying the painting. That's a start. And he's not usually a tough guy to find—have you tried calling him?" The edge in my voice was condescending and I knew it. "Sorry. I'm just—"

"Overcaffeinated," Kyle said as he walked in. "Max told me

you were guzzling java like there was no tomorrow, and obviously he wasn't lying."

"Have to stay awake; can't let that thing get ahold of me again." I caught myself biting the inside of my lip.

"About that." Jake picked up the coffee cup he'd been rinsing out when I pounced on him. "I talked with your mom. She says whoever was in your dream was most likely a mage of some sort. They can walk in different realities as easily as we do in this one."

I remembered what Aunt Juliet had said about accidentally slipping into Kildenren's dream, and they had made babies. So it was perfectly logical that this person could kill me in mine. "That's not making me feel any better."

"I wish I had better news, and for the record we did call Emilio. We also have men checking all of his usual haunts."

I held up a shaky hand. "Thanks. I'm—not going to say I'm sorry again." I laughed. "Jeez. If I take your head off, guys, just roll with it. You know I don't mean anything. It's the coffee talking."

They both chuckled and made for the door.

"Oh, your mother wanted me to tell you that a council meeting has been called and they are on high alert." Jake ran from the room after he said it. Kyle must have understood the impact the words would have on me, because he booked it, too.

Chickens.

High alert meant that the council members needed us to protect them while they met. Ack.

"Can't you tell them we're busy?" I complained to my mother.

"Gillian," she admonished. I'd found her searching for something in her personal library. "You know it doesn't work that way. You were born to protect the universe from harm." She turned to look at me. "You look like the walking dead." She glanced down at her watch. "Take two hours to rest. It will take us that long to prepare everything for the journey."

"Mom, I can't sleep. Whatever it is that has Bailey tried to kill me in my sleep. Besides that, he is still missing, and now with this we have even less time to look for him."

"I'm quite aware that my son is gone. What you must realize is that you are no good to any of us if you aren't at full power, Gillian. I can do a spell that will protect you while you rest, and we'll make sure that someone is there to watch you."

"Mom, I'm not going to sleep. I almost died. You're powerful and I realize it probably wouldn't matter much to you if I died, but I'm not willing to take the chance with my life."

Her hand smacked against my cheek so hard it jarred my brain. "Don't you ever say anything so stupid again, young lady. You and your sisters are my world. Do you understand that? You were born to protect the universe, and you have important jobs, but you will always be my daughters."

I rubbed my cheek. "Damn, Mom. You must be working out again. That hurt."

She rolled her eyes. "I lost my temper. Events—well, you

know it's all a bit much. When I tell you I can protect you from the darkness, you need to believe me." She handed me some pills. "These are herbs that will help you sleep for a short time. When you wake you'll feel refreshed."

I'd been dismissed but I wasn't ready to go. I needed her to listen to me. "Mom. These murders—the ones here and in Paris—they have something to do with me and I'm afraid Bailey's going to die because I couldn't kill the demon king. If my brother dies, I will never be able to forgive myself."

"Enough!" my mother yelled. I jerked back, afraid she might hit me again.

"You are not the reason your brother has been taken. The darkness is rising, Gillian. Evil is the reason your brother is gone. It has absolutely nothing to do with you; someone only wants you to think that."

The power roiled off her in waves, and she took a deep breath. "The shifts, your brother, the sudden upheaval and breaking of treaties. Those things are related, but none of them have anything to do with you. As a Guardian you must put duty in front of everything else. If you had killed the demon king, that entire world would be after you, as well as its allies. There would be little we could do to keep them from destroying you and the rest of us.

"Evil, Gillian. Evil has everything to do with this. You made the right choice by not killing Arath. Though I could wring your neck for reuniting him and Juliet."

The sudden shift in topic threw me off guard. I knew she

wasn't in the mood, but I had to ask. "Why were they kept apart? You knew, didn't you?"

"Yes, I knew. It was best for all involved if Juliet believed her children gone. They would have been in constant danger here. We were facing much the same thing as we are now, and back then Maunra, though more barbaric than Earth, was simply safer. Arath also needed to learn the old ways of magic from beings that aren't welcome on Earth. The demon king has a great destiny, one that could only be fulfilled if he was raised on Maunra. His father understood the sacrifice, and I believe Arath does, too."

"I don't understand."

My mother sighed. "Gillian, when we get back I will do my best to explain. Right now I must concentrate on working protection spells to keep us alive at the summit. Please go and rest. In a few hours all of you girls must be at maximum power. We are going into a very dangerous situation." She moved away from me and picked up a book. "And I'm sorry I slapped you. I took an oath to harm none, and I'm not pleased with myself for hitting my own daughter. That wasn't one of my finest moments."

Before I left the room I walked over and kissed her cheek. She wasn't perfect, but she was my mother and I loved her. I'd never seen her lose her temper, but this situation had bested all of us.

* * *

Back in my room I made some notes about what we might need for the council meeting. There was no way I'd fall asleep again, at least not until we'd rounded up all the bad guys. I wouldn't risk taking the herbs my mother had given me.

My brain cells were out of whack and I couldn't concentrate. I wondered if Arath had survived the battle. I couldn't imagine him ever losing anything, but the uncertainty over what had happened to him gnawed at my insides. *Please, God, let him be alive. I'd like one more chance to tell him that I'm sorry.* Damn, I'd said that a lot the last couple of hours.

I wished Arath could be at the council meeting. The way things were going we needed someone with that kind of power.

There was a knock on the door. "Time to gear up. We leave in twenty." Mira pointed at her watch.

I yawned and stretched. "Do you have any of those herbs you used to give me during exams?" I told her about the dream and what had happened.

"I'll have something ready for you in the weapons room. You won't need to sleep for a week, and you won't get nervous like you do when you're overcaffeinated." When she noticed my hands shaking, she frowned. "How much coffee have you had?"

"Is it possible to have too much?" I joked, but it wasn't funny.

"Jeez, you're going to burn out your nervous system. I'll take care of that problem, too. Meet me downstairs." She shut the door.

Council meetings were volatile at best, as representatives from all the worlds would be there. They didn't necessarily get a vote, but they wanted their voices heard.

That meant we had to not only gear up, but also armor up. Guardians were responsible for protecting the council members from physical harm, and we were also supposed to be neutral peacekeepers. Someone always wanted to start trouble, and it was our job to make sure that didn't happen.

I met everyone in the weapons room. All of us wore the same thing, white T-shirt with leather jacket and pants. Underneath the shirt was armor fitted to our bodies made out of material that would keep a sword from piercing our hearts, but was also easy to move in. It was another of Bailey's inventions.

I will find you, little brother. I sent my thought out to the universe in the hopes he might hear me.

My mother had gone ahead.

Mira handed me a small container. "Chug this. It tastes like crap, but it works immediately."

She didn't lie. It tasted like dirt mixed with wheatgrass, but I felt the energy as it zinged through my body. At the same time my breathing slowed and I felt the caffeine edge die down. "Damn, that's good stuff." I shook my head.

"When I'm out in the jungle, I don't like to sleep either," Mira said as she put one of Bailey's blasters in a holster at her hip. "Never know what kind of creepy crawlies will make their way into your tent."

"You could make a fortune selling this stuff to college

students during midterms and finals." I took a deep calming breath and my body felt like it was back to normal.

Mira laughed. "Those herbs are not easy to find, so we won't be mass-producing it anytime soon."

"Well, I think we could all use a little bottle of it," Alex said. "The last few days none of us has had much sleep."

"Are you ready?" Claire glanced back at me as the portal opened.

I nodded. "Let's get this over with."

CHAPTER
28

Two minutes later we landed outside the council chambers. The hall was empty now, but in a half hour the place would crawl with beings from every world imaginable. I could feel the protective wards my mother had set. They would make it much easier for us to spot trouble, but we also had a lot to do before everyone arrived.

"Alex, check the perimeter."

As the oldest, I was the lead in these situations. No one had ever said otherwise; it had always been that way.

"Claire, stash the weapons so that we have easy access. Mira, take a peek out at the crowd and see what we're dealing with. I'm going to check out the conference area." They nodded. The weapons would be placed in strategic areas, so that we would have access no matter where we were in the crowd.

These meetings were held on neutral planets called Prats. They were used for this purpose only, to provide a meeting place where no world was in control. A few beings inhabited the planet in small villages all under the jurisdiction of the council. They were responsible for the upkeep of the buildings used for the conferences.

When the actual meeting took place, the Guardians would stand alongside the members' personal bodyguards.

The lyceum seated more than a thousand. I sighed. *It's too damn big.* A stage with a heavy stone council table had been set. The thing was transported to each venue. It was made of a healing stone that promoted peace. From what I'd seen at these events, the council needed all the peace-promoting help it could get.

Surrounded by high-backed chairs, it looked like an enormous dining room table. A podium took center stage. The various council members would take turns speaking if necessary. I'd been to meetings that had taken several days to complete. I prayed that didn't happen with this one. We needed to get back home. I knew Kyle and Jake were doing their best to find Bailey, but I'd feel much better if I were there instead of here.

We all would. Mira's thought came into my head. *Stay focused, Gilly. Let's get through this.*

I smiled. She was up and running on full power. It was time for me to do the same. I took a deep cleansing breath and brought my shoulders to my ears, stretching my arms far above my head.

Clearing my mind, I tried to get a sense of the room. Claire came in with a sweeper. It's a great device that can detect explosives from more than two hundred yards away. She held it up as she walked down the center of the lyceum.

From her pocket she pulled something out and threw it at me. "We need special comms, because of the magic. Alex grabbed these just before we left and stuffed them in my pocket. They are also magicproof, so if someone tries to use magic to keep us from communicating, it won't work. Of course, we also have our secret weapon, Mira."

We all nodded in agreement.

"Alex or Mira sense anything outside?"

"No, but the crowd is gathering. Mom sent Mira a message. They'll be entering from the back. That way we don't have to worry about crowd protection until they get in here. Five minutes left for prep, then they're letting them in."

There were two side rooms off the stage, and I checked to make sure they were empty.

My nerves were on edge, and they'd stay that way until this was over. Creating trouble or even making threats during a council meeting meant instant death to anyone who dared. That's how we'd always been able to keep the peace for hundreds of years. Cause trouble and you die at the hands of a Guardian. It made it simple and the beings who came to these events knew the rules.

Of course, that didn't keep the occasional idiot from making some kind of move. It had been a few years since anyone had tried anything. Call it instinct, but I had my doubts about this meeting going off without a hitch.

I'm with you on that, sister, Mira said in my mind. *Alex and I are coming in. It's about to begin.*

They both moved through the center aisle and we took our places in front of the stage. We were the first line of defense, with the other guards right behind us.

The door opened at the back of the platform and the guards filed in with the council members following behind them.

My neck tingled and my senses went into overdrive. Something was wrong. I motioned to Claire and she nodded.

I moved up the steps to see the crowd on the stage more clearly. That's when I saw him.

Arath stood at the head of the conference table, and gave me a look that would kill most mortals.

CHAPTER

29

He's alive. Before I could even process the information that Arath had survived the battle he'd been in the last time I saw him, the meeting was called to order. My heart raced. *Thank you, God.* I sent up a silent prayer. It didn't look like he was interested in talking to me anytime soon. It didn't matter. I still had a chance to make him forgive me. *He looks damn good.* I glanced at him again.

"Get your head in the game," Mira said into the comm. "You can fawn all over Hot Stuff later."

"I don't know how much fawning there's going to be," added Alex. "Did you see that look he gave her? Scary."

"Shut up and get to work," I whispered. I couldn't help taking one last look back. God, he was even more handsome than the last time I saw him. The council robes were nothing but large tents, but Arath made it look like a hot new trend.

Marcel was the first to speak, since he was the one to call the meeting to order. "We are going to relax council rules just this once in an effort to get the necessary information out as quickly as possible.

"I will speak for the rest of the council regarding our stance with the problems on Xerxes, as well as the dark magic that is infiltrating our planets.

"Many of you know this same thing happened to my world many years ago. This is an evil we must all join together to fight. We saw what happened on Xerxes when they tried to handle the situation on their own."

A few crowd members grumbled. Looked like we had a few dragons in the audience, but no one made a move.

"We are working with the leaders of each world to put wards in place to help protect against the evil. This is not a permanent solution, but it will give us time to gather our armies to fight."

A huge blast shook the building. There was a stunned silence for one second, and then people screamed and the entire crowd began moving our way.

"Security breach in the hall," Alex shouted.

"Mom," Claire shouted, "get them out of here." She motioned to the council.

Another bomb blasted behind us. "We're surrounded. Mira, open a portal and get them out of here," I shouted as I ran to cover the back stage door to keep the intruders out. The bomb had been close enough that my ears rang.

"Save your strength." Arath pushed Mira to the side. "Protect the flanks. *Gorstat!*" He shouted and a portal opened in the center of the stage. "Go," he ordered the rest of the members, just as the doors all around burst open.

Crowds of creatures ran screaming into the room, most hysterical, trying to get away from what was happening outside.

The guards and my sisters formed a tight band around the stage, as the members walked into the portal one by one.

An arrow came out of nowhere straight toward my head. I caught it in the air.

"To the left. Fifteen yards," Alex yelled as she shot a fierce-looking being with the head of camel and the body of a human.

"Clorde soldiers." Claire motioned to the back of the hall. These were mercenaries. Soldiers for hire, whose sole purpose was to kill.

"Oh, hell." I moved to fighting stance, and my sisters did the same.

The soldiers advanced without regard for anything in their path. Their swords swung with abandon as they moved toward us. I shoved my gun in my holster as I pulled out my saber.

Claire and Mira used their Magnums—they both loved

guns way more than I did—as we tightened the band. I glanced back quickly to see that only three of the council members had crossed through. Some were insisting on staying to fight. Many of them were warriors on their planets, and warriors never left a fight.

"Mom, tell them we can handle it. Get them the hell out of here. We're going to need them to protect their worlds."

I saw her shove several members toward the light. "Your day to fight will come," she yelled at them. "Go!"

Obviously they were as intimidated by her as the rest of us were, for they moved faster.

"Gilly, look out." I turned in time to catch another arrow, which narrowly missed my cheek. In the short time I'd looked away, the Clordes had advanced even farther. The innocents in the room seemed to sense what was about to happen and began running for the doors from which they'd just arrived.

The first camel-headed creature reached me just as I pulled out my sword. Metal clanged twice before his head fell to the ground at his feet, the body still standing. We held our position and let them advance, mowing them down as they did. The idiots didn't seem bright enough to turn and run.

The room smelled of blood and death. The hordes of Clordes kept coming, and it didn't seem as if the battle would end anytime soon. *How the hell had they been allowed through security?* It was a question for another day. I had to concentrate on killing them one by one. I sensed my sisters doing the same.

"Council is clear," I heard one of the guards say behind me.

Out of the corner of my eye I saw Mom in her long gold robe. "Mom, get out of here," I shouted to her, but as I did an arrow flew toward her. "Watch out," I screamed. In an effort to run to her I'd turned my back on my quarry and his sword came down hard on my back. The armor kept the thing from slicing through, but the force behind it knocked the breath out of me and I fell forward. I pulled my body into a roll and jumped up. I swung my sword around and divested the creature of its head.

I chanced another look back but didn't see Mom. *Good, she's out.*

Enough of this crap. I pulled the guns Bailey had made. We'd never used them in this type of situation, but it seemed appropriate.

Yanking back the triggers, I charged the weapons. When the light turned green, I let loose. The plasma ray mowed down twenty Clordes in less than a minute.

Alex saw what I did, and she pulled out her guns, too. In less than ten minutes it was Clordes zero, Caruthers sisters at least one hundred.

We were bloody and covered in muck, but we'd survived. The guards who had been standing behind us moved forward to make certain there were no more of the mercenaries.

"God bless Bailey," Alex said as she stuffed her guns back in her holsters. "I was afraid to use these things like that. We're lucky they didn't blow up."

"No joke." I let out a tired laugh.

"Gillian." I heard Arath's voice behind me. He didn't call me Guardian, and I was pleased—until I turned to see what he wanted.

Mom was in his arms, an arrow sticking out of her chest.

CHAPTER

30

"Mom," Claire cried out.

As Arath carefully situated Mom on the council table, we ran to her. "The arrow will not budge. It's surrounded by dark magic." He frowned, and I realized the situation was dire.

"You're so strong, Arath. You can do it. Save her, please," I urged him.

"No." Mom's voice was weak with pain. "The poison is already in my bloodstream. If he pulls it out the wound will heal and I'll become one of them." She pointed a finger toward the Clordes. "I must die, or become the thing I detest the most."

"You're wrong, Mom. Arath is powerful far beyond anything I've ever seen. He can do it. Please, let him help you."

I leaned across the table and grabbed her hand. We'd had our differences, but I loved her. We all did. "Mom, please, you have to let him."

"I'm not his biggest fan," added Alex, "but if he can save you—"

"Please," Claire choked out. "We can't lose you, too."

Mira nodded.

Mom stared up at Arath. "Do you know the old ways?"

"Savnon trained me in the old ways of spells and herbs."

Even near death she managed a small smile. "He's still alive? I thought he died in the Blood Wars." She coughed and blood spewed from her mouth. "If you don't do the spell correctly, you know what will happen."

He nodded.

"Are you prepared to kill me?" She gave him her best steely stare, one that generally sent the rest of us packing.

"If necessary," he told her.

What?

She waved her hand around at us. "Girls, promise me you will let Arath do what he must. If the spell doesn't work, he must end me before darkness takes over."

Claire sobbed. "Mom, you aren't going to die."

Mom looked over at me. "Gillian, you must make sure he is allowed to do it. I will not rise with this darkness inside of me. Do you understand?"

I bit the inside of my lip to keep from crying. "Yes." I was the oldest and I had to be the strong one. It had always been this way. That didn't stop me from feeling like a big blubbery baby.

Arath moved so that he was next to her. "You must clear the area. It is best if you do not look. It will be painful for her, as I rid her body of the toxins."

He took off his council robe, revealing his jeans and T-shirt underneath. Pulling a small vial from a pouch at his hip, he held it to her lips. "This will help some with the pain," he told my mother, "but I have nothing to prepare you for the fire you are about to feel."

Mom nodded. "Do what you must, Arath. I am in your debt."

"Alex and Claire, go gather our weapons from the hall," I ordered. "Mira, keep a check on the front doors." They all wanted to argue, I could see it in their eyes, but they didn't. They moved away to do as I asked.

"I want to help you." I stared at Arath.

"It is not wise. The pain will be immense." His hands were over her head. Mom cried out.

"Please don't let her die," I whispered as I turned to cover the back doors. Arath was right, I couldn't watch her writhe in pain. It was too much to see this strong woman I'd loved all my life grow weaker by the second. She was so proud, and this was no way for her to die.

Arath chanted a healing spell, and the magic came off of him in waves. *He's so powerful. He can do this.* I tried to convince myself. The room glowed with his magic, and I hoped my mother's eyes were closed so she didn't singe her retinas.

I knew the moment he pulled the arrow from her chest. She gasped and coughed, a horrible hacking sound. I sent my own healing chants toward her. I didn't have that much magic in me for this sort of thing, but I could give her what I had.

Ten minutes later Arath stopped, and the light dimmed. I glanced back. Mom's normally tan skin was a grayish white. Her body had stopped moving and I feared she'd died.

Arath's power rose and glowed again, in much the same way he had when we had closed the portals. I turned my face away, and waited. The heat of his magic reached me and warmed my body.

God, please let her live. I promise I'll be a better daughter. We need her. The glow dimmed again and I turned to see Arath shaking his head.

I took the few steps so that I could touch her. "What happened? She's so cold."

"Your mother is a great warrior and she fights for her life. Her will is strong, but I've done all I can. It's up to her now." He didn't take his eyes from her and I knew he really had done all he could. He wanted her to live as much as we did.

"She's not breathing." I noticed her chest didn't rise. The tears fell on my cheeks.

Arath moved behind me and put his hands on my shoulders. "She is between death and life, but she breathes. It's shallow."

My sisters were back in the lyceum. I felt them before I saw them. "Stay where you are," I ordered them. "We can't know what she will be when she wakes up." If my mother was afraid of becoming an evil thing, then I knew it had to be bad. If Arath did have to kill her, well, I didn't want to have to fight my own sisters. They were warriors but I wasn't certain they were strong enough to let Arath kill our mother if necessary.

I turned to look up at Arath. "How long until we know? Is she going to wake up?"

As I said the words my mother sat straight up, gasping for air. Arath pulled me away from her and threw me to the back of the stage.

"Mage. Do you fight for the darkness?" he roared. His eyes were a fiery orange and he turned into big red scary Arath in less than a second.

She didn't answer.

Oh, crap.

Arath pulled his knife from the sheath at his back. "Mage, do you fight for the dark? I command you to speak." The knife wasn't visible to her and she continued to stare ahead. Then her eyes closed and her head dropped.

"I am a warrior for the light. Sworn to uphold the true magic of the universe. I am love," she whispered.

My arms tingled with the words and I felt my mother's magic wash over me. I couldn't stop the sobs. We all ran to her, and she took us in her arms. I don't remember many hugs from my mother. Oh, there were a few. When we were ill, or as we went through the levels of becoming a Guardian, she gave us brief pats on the back at the ceremonies. But she wasn't the kind of mom who was generous with the affection.

Except for today. She held on to each of us as if her life depended on it.

Finally she looked at Arath. "I thank you for the great gift you have given me today." She bowed her head to him. I'd never seen her do that in the presence of anyone.

"Wise warrior, it is your gift"—he waved a hand to take in all of us—"that saved this from being a great tragedy. Your Guardians have served us well. Now you must go home to your healers."

She nodded.

Arath opened a portal in much the same way he had for the council. "She is weak. Call my mother to her, and she will know what to do," he instructed.

I picked my mom up off the table and cradled her in my arms.

"I don't know how to thank you." A single tear slipped down my cheek. Yesterday I'd gone to Maunra intent on murdering him, and today he had saved my mother.

I am a terrible, awful person, and he's never going to forgive me.

He frowned. "She saved my life once. Now I have returned the favor. The debt is paid, Guardian." His eyes were cold now. I knew he was thinking about the last time we'd seen one another. "You must go." It was an order.

"Arath, I'm sorry. I wouldn't—" I needed to explain to him

that I cared for him. Everyone stared at me. I couldn't do this in front of them. It was too personal. The way he stared at me, I had a feeling he never wanted to see me again. The idea of that made my heart hurt in my chest. "It's just that, you know, I had to—"

My mom raised her head and gave me a withering glance. I couldn't tell if it was because of the pain, or the fact I'd botched my apology again.

"You—just, thank you for what you did today. I can never repay you. I'm sorry. I seem to be saying that a lot lately, but you have to know how much—"

Arath's face was blank of emotion. "You must go."

"Gilly, we have to get Mom back. You heard what he said." Claire pulled on my shoulder. "Mom needs to get to the healers and we have to find Aunt Juliet."

Alex whispered in my ear, "Besides, you sound like a moron."

I rolled my eyes.

"Thank you," my sisters said in unison as they pushed me toward the portal.

I pulled Mom tight to my chest and walked to the light, wondering if I would ever see Arath again.

CHAPTER

31

A day later we were no closer to finding Bailey, but my mother had healed at an amazing rate. It was a good thing, since whoever wielded the dark magic wasn't interested in taking a holiday. We'd been fighting it for the last twenty-four hours.

There had been a rash of demon and dragon jumpers. Most of them only used our world to jump to the next. It seemed like everyone was trying to get the hell out of Dodge. Unfortunately, no place was safe. We had the occasional demon or dragon that wanted to lag behind, which kept us busy. While Alex and I were off fighting, Mira and Claire looked after Mom and followed up on leads concerning our brother.

After a particularly bloody battle just outside of Buenos

Aires with a demon that had landed in the middle of a polo match, I was ready for a shower and a change of clothes.

"What happened?" Mira asked. She stood in the doorway of my bathroom while I showered.

"Damn thing ripped jewels right off the necks of the women with its teeth." I scrubbed the last of the ooze from my hair with the vanilla shampoo, then applied conditioner. "People were running and screaming. It had four legs so they thought it was some kind of mutated horse, thank God. You wouldn't believe the chaos."

"Oh, I would." Mira handed me a bathrobe as I opened the door. There wasn't much modesty in our family. I think there seldom is with sisters who have grown up together.

"Alex says she ran into the same sort of thing in Mexico City, only her dragons were in their human form. They weren't after treasure, though. At least, she doesn't think so. They were more interested in some strange book at the museum. Had to do with artifacts."

I sighed as I wrapped a towel around my wet hair. "It's all the same to them. I wanted to speak to Arath about it. I noticed some of the jewelry from the Vatican on his altar there. I know he didn't steal it, but I never remembered to ask him why it was there."

Which gave me the perfect excuse to go to Maunra and ask him about it.

"Did you by chance find any answers about the Amol demons Arath mentioned?"

Mira sat on the edge of my bed while I applied styling gel to my hair. "Yes, well, I didn't, Claire did. The Manteros use the Amols to do their dirty work just like Arath said."

"I'd never heard of the Manteros until he mentioned them. What the hell are they?"

"It's one of those idiot secret societies that serve the dark. It's made up of all kinds of creatures and even humans and mages. Bunch of creeps if you ask me. Mom's certain they're behind all of this crap. This isn't the first time, like Marcel said. They've been able to destroy entire worlds.

"The Amols are able to adapt to whatever world they are in, so they can slip in and do what's necessary without being noticed. Sneaky bastards." Mira leaned back on the bed.

"So why did they take Bailey?" I looked at her reflection in the mirror.

"Mom thinks it was to distract us."

"From what?"

She shrugged. "Well, I'm not sure we were all on our A-game at the council meeting. I mean, we all survived, but I wonder if we hadn't been so tired and distracted from the few days before, if perhaps we would have been more tuned in. You know me. When I'm on full power, I don't miss things like bombs. They were just outside the building. If it weren't for the facts that the place was made of indestructible stone, and that it was protected by Mom's magic, we'd all be dead."

I frowned. "Is he still alive, Mira?"

She knew what I meant. "I believe he is. I can't connect with him, but I don't feel that sense of loss. Remember when Dad died? Even though I was light-years away, I knew what had happened."

I moved to the closet to find something to wear. "So these Manteros. Are they behind the darkness? Did they unleash whatever it is?"

"Yes and no. Mom doesn't think they'd be strong enough on their own, so they had to have help. She calls it the Source, which sounds like something off an old *Buffy* episode. If we could find the Source, then we could find a way to stop it."

I leaned my head against the door frame of the closet. "I don't know about you, but this is just too much for me right now. I can't seem to get my mind around it."

She walked over to me. "I hate that it changes everything. We worked hard before, but it's going to get worse before it gets better." She put a hand on my shoulder.

"Jeez, Mira, always with the good news." Alex stood in the doorway dressed in a pair of jeans and T-shirt.

"Hey. I heard you've been having as much fun as I have." I held up my arm that sported a long line of stitches where a demon blade had sliced through.

Alex rolled her eyes. "Oh, yes. I was the most popular girl at the dance. Unfortunately, none of the boys I was with made it home." She gave an evil smirk.

"That's why you never have a second date," I joked. "You're always killing them the first time you meet."

Alex snorted. "Mom wants to see you. Oh, Mira, Jake says there's a message for you." She held up a hand. "It's not Fae related, it's business."

"Thank God." She pulled Alex's hair as she walked by. "I'll talk to you two later."

Alex yawned. "I'm going to catch a quick nap and then see what I can do to help Jake and Kyle. Claire's in the control room with both of them, so if there's news she'll let us know." She waved good-bye.

I slipped on a pair of yoga pants and a knit top, but left my feet bare.

I was glad Mom wanted to talk to me. I had something very important I needed to ask her.

Mom sat at her desk in the sitting room just outside her bedroom. She didn't bother turning toward the door when she heard me. The desk was piled high with books, and she was in the middle of taking copious notes.

"Have a seat, Gillian. I'll be a moment." She pointed to the comfy chair next to the fireplace. As I sat down and crossed my legs beneath me, the fire roared to life.

I'd always been in awe of my mother's magic, and she never failed to surprise me. She hadn't changed anything in here since my dad had died. His desk was as he left it on the opposite side of the room. While it was regularly dusted, nothing was ever actually moved out of place. Even though my mother had complained many times that their sitting room felt like something at a men's club, with the rich dark wood walls and floors, and soft leather chairs, she had done nothing to make it more feminine.

I always believed it was her way of preserving what she had with my dad. I never understood their relationship. My mother had always been a force to be reckoned with, but Dad had a way of handling her. She'd never smiled much, but he'd always managed to tease one of out of her when she was in one of her moods.

When she'd finished with her task she turned to me.

"Have you notified Arath about the jumpers?"

I shook my head. "No, they didn't come from Maunra. Jake said they dimension-jumped from somewhere else. I didn't see the need to bother the demon king."

"Hmmm." Her face was a mask and I couldn't read her.

"Mom, there's something I've wanted to ask you." I shifted uncomfortably in my chair. I think perhaps because I wasn't sure I wanted to hear the answer.

"Stop fidgeting, Gillian. You're a grown woman, a protector of Earth, you can ask me a simple question."

I took a deep breath. "That's just it. The question isn't that simple."

"You want to know why I bowed to Arath?"

I gasped with surprise. "How did you know?"

"I saw the look on your face when I thanked him. The bow

was a sign of respect to an incredibly powerful mage. The truth is I've never seen a male mage with so much power."

I'd suspected the same, but my jaw almost hit my chest.

She smiled. "You've already witnessed what he could do when you closed the portals with him. That kind of power comes along perhaps once in a century, and we haven't seen anyone with Arath's talents in several centuries. He's what we call a Nokoron. While most of us have talents in certain areas, he is good at all of it."

"A Nokoron?" Overwhelmed didn't begin to describe how I felt. "Mother, I've done an inordinate amount of reading about everything to do with our world and the universe. I've never heard of a Nokoron."

She nodded. "They are only written about in the old text. And I told you it has been several hundred years since we saw the last one that had powers like this. I'd suspected as much when you told us about how he guided you through the portals and then the Vex. It takes an enormous amount of strength to do that. But I knew for certain when he pulled the darkness from me. Only one who is pure light can do that. If it had not been for him, I would be dead."

"Please don't say that," I begged her. "We may not always agree, but I can't stand the idea of you being gone."

She smiled. "You also want to know why we lied to Juliet."

"We?"

"Your father and I. Juliet had her children here, in this

home. We knew when they were born that they were both special. Throe doesn't have the power the demon king does, but he has great strength. Your father knew when he held Arath what he was. He made the deal with Arath's father. As a child the boy would have been in constant danger here. Even though he looked human, it was to be several years before he could control his talents. We were in an all-out war with the darkness here, and it was before the portals were locked with magic. If someone found out about Arath, they would have done anything to kill him. He's powerful now, and his strength will only continue to grow. As I said, he has quite a future ahead, and we had to make sure that he had the opportunity to have one."

"But wasn't there somewhere better than Maunra to raise such a special child? And why did you let Aunt Juliet think he was dead?"

Mom took another long breath. "She understands now, but she wouldn't have then. She was so headstrong and she loved her babies. On Maunra, there are fewer portals, and Arath's father wasn't without his own talents. He had the power to read minds, which is why he was such a great warrior. He also had the strength of forty demons. In his world, children are raised by a village, and protected as one would a treasure. There was no safer place than Maunra for those children.

"After Juliet had her first few visits with the children there, we knew that things were not going to work out as we planned.

Your father stumbled upon her plot to kidnap them and take them to another world. That's when we decided it would be best if she believed them dead."

I'd never seen my mother cry, but a single tear slid down her cheek. "One of the hardest things I've ever had to do in service to the universe is to keep Juliet from her children. It broke my heart."

I moved to her and took her hands. "You did what you thought was best."

Sighing, she shook her head. "I did what I knew was best for those children. They have grown into magnificent beings. Juliet was furious with me the other night, but she understands. She may not talk to me anytime soon, but she understands."

I didn't blame my aunt.

"Mom, I know we don't talk about these things, but I have feelings for Arath. Finding out he's so powerful changes everything."

She stared up at me. "He will not be an easy man to love, but he is a man. Yes, he holds great power, but he is a true leader of the light. You could not wish for a better soul."

I shook my head. "A demon with a soul. There's something terribly wrong with that."

I rubbed my temples as I left my mother's room. I needed a long nap. Three or four days would do it, but I decided a good bit of seated meditation was a better idea. Since we hadn't exactly extinguished the evil yet.

As I sat staring at the flame, the tears flowed. Not just for Aunt Juliet and Arath, a mother and child separated for the greater good.

No, my tears were selfish.

I was in love with one powerful mage, and I was certain he hated me.

CHAPTER
32

I was in my room trying to catch up on the multitude of paperwork when Jake called my cell phone. "We have multiple jumpers, and we've tracked Bailey to where they landed."

"What? Never mind. I'm on my way." Making a quick stop at my closet I grabbed some leather pants and a jacket to throw over my black knit top. Then I took off at a dead run for the control room.

Jake stood with my sword and two of the laser guns at the ready. "They're just outside Sun Valley, Idaho, on a mountain. We've set in the coordinates for you." He handed me the watch. "They sent a message. You are to come alone, or they'll kill Bailey."

I nodded. "Don't tell my sisters; I don't want to do anything that might jeopardize Bailey's life."

He's alive. Jake wouldn't have seen him on the control panel if Bailey weren't still breathing. I didn't care who I had to kill—my brother would come home tonight.

Jake frowned. "Mira will know as soon as you put those tattoos together. She probably already does."

"It's your job to stall her. Tell her to give me a half hour. If I'm not back they can all come through."

"I'll try, but you know how they are. If they want to come after you I can't stop them." He handed me my sword.

A few seconds later, I stood in a foot of snow outside an abandoned cabin. The windows had been boarded up, but there were fresh tracks. Pulling out my sword I moved around the perimeter, stepping as lightly as possible.

"Welcome, Guardian." A voice came out from the trees to my left. It sounded vaguely familiar. The English words were spoken with a slight accent, but I couldn't tell if it was Italian or Spanish.

"Give me my brother." I moved into an attack position. "I know he's here."

"Oh, but you did not honor the agreement. I thought it would be much more fun if you could watch him die." A light flashed on and I saw Bailey tied to a tree. They had a gag in his mouth and the bald-headed Amols had him surrounded.

Shouldn't be a problem.

I was so grateful to see him alive I could have killed a hundred demons to save him. They'd done a number on his face and his arms were bloody. My little brother had put up a fight. He blinked and I looked down to see his hand move in one of our private signals.

His fingers told me that he was okay, and that he wanted me to kill the bastards. Well, I added that last bit, but knowing he was okay gave me even more strength.

"The demon king was in the middle of a battle. There was no way I could get to him."

The voice laughed. "Lies. Clede tells me you were in the king's rooms before the war and had every opportunity to kill Arath."

"Clede is mistaken." The jerk was a traitor to Arath. "I did go to the castle, but the king was not there."

"You lie," Clede bellowed and stepped out from the trees.

"Traitor," I yelled back. "Arath trusted you."

"He is a half-breed. Not fit to rule our world."

"Well, you're a racist pig." Okay, that wasn't the most mature thing to say since he did look like a warthog had been his mother.

He leapt into the middle of the snow a foot from where I stood. *Jeez, that guy can jump.* The thought sifted through my head as my sword came up ready for battle. His left claw came for my throat and I ducked. My left leg shot out for a knee but I miscalculated and threw myself off balance. *Crap.* His other paw came down and landed a blow to my right jaw, which made me see tiny black specks float in my eyes.

He wore a piece of armor against his chest so it was impossible to get to his heart. There was only one way to kill him.

I shifted my weight and moved to the side of him. I felt a sharp pain in my left shoulder. A quick look back told me I'd been shot with some kind of dart. Poison, I could already feel it working its way into my bloodstream.

Damn.

"Bailey, the jerks don't fight fair. They shot me with poison." Reaching back, I pulled the dart from my shoulder and then went after the demons. Time was of the essence and I had to kill these idiots so Bailey could get home.

A swift kick to his snout sent Clede flying across the snow, leaving a trail of green goo and blood.

The evil laugh rattled the branches of the barren trees. What they didn't know was my metabolism wasn't like other people's. I moved toward Bailey, determined to cut him free before I died.

He blinked twice and I remembered the guns at my sides. As the Amols made their move, I pulled one out. They were no longer a problem.

Clede didn't cooperate. I smashed his nose even farther into his face, but he had at least a foot in height on me and another hundred pounds. We were matched in strength, though. The gun jammed or ran out of plasma, and he knocked it out of my hand. I didn't have time to pull out the other one before his claw came toward my head.

I dove past him and dug my bowie into the cartilage of his knee. He stumbled and I moved to the tree and sliced Bailey free with one swath of the knife. He yanked his gag off. "Gilly," he screamed and we both ducked. Clede's sword came down against the tree.

I caught a movement to the right of me—the man behind the voice. I threw Bailey the second of the guns. "Tag, you're it," I yelled, and looked in the direction where I'd heard the dark laugh.

Bailey held the gun up like Clint Eastwood ready to shoot anything that came near. Clede struck out again, but this time his sword hit dead center in my back. The point sliced through to the right of my spine, the pain taking any breath I had left.

"Only a coward strikes from behind." I'd whispered, but he heard me. He pulled the blade out ready to do it again and I turned, slicing through the air with determination. Clede's head tumbled from his shoulders before the rest of him could react.

"No." I heard a shifting sound to my right and another demon approached. This one was smaller, possibly female. Most likely, Clede's mate. She stumbled to his body, and then turned fierce yellow eyes on me. Before I could even think, she was vaporized.

Bailey stood behind me. The laser gun glowed in his hand.

"That thing is damn cool. You should have seen how well it worked when we were attacked at the council meeting." I tried to smile but the poison and the wound had taken their toll.

I didn't have much time. *Mira, hurry. Save Bailey.* I sent my thoughts to her, praying she heard them.

Someone clapped behind us. I turned to see Emilio. No wonder the voice sounded familiar. "I am one of many," he said. His eyes blazed, then became inky black.

Bailey pointed the gun.

"You're not smart enough to have masterminded all of this," I sneered.

"No? Not as the being you see before you, but *I* can *do* many things. I can *be* many things." The eyes on the creature swirled. Whatever this thing was, it wasn't Emilio.

"How long have you possessed him? Are you responsible for the murders?"

He laughed and it was pure evil. "I used your Emilio to do some of my dirty work, but I have many minions. It does not end here, Guardian. My kind will destroy this place soon, and there's nothing you can do about it."

I fell to my knees, unable to stand, and Bailey dropped the gun to catch me. Emilio jumped forward to grab the weapon and I brought my sword up through his jaw and the top of his head.

The thing screeched and then fell straight back. The immediate threat was over.

I coughed and my lungs were on fire. My body shook, and I knew death was on the way. "Bailey, tell them all I love them. I'll miss you." I coughed again, and he helped to keep my head out of the snow as I fell to the side. Blood splattered on his chest.

"So cold. Arath, I need your warmth."

My mind drifted to that one night when he held me close and we danced. A perfect moment, I had one to remember always.

Then there was nothing but inky blackness.

CHAPTER

33

A shadow loomed before me, large and menacing. It was in the shape of a man, and it was so big it blocked the light I'd been trying to follow in my dream. *This isn't what I thought heaven would be.* Suddenly a thought occurred to me. *Crap, I've screwed up my karma and I'm going the wrong way.*

"It isn't time for your soul to go, Gillian." Arath's voice boomed in my ears. "Come back to me."

Arath? What is he doing here?

Before the thought could fully materialize, my body was sucked through a vacuum so strong it felt as if my bones were being crushed in a trash compactor. A whirl of colors flashed before my eyes. The pain was so intense I screamed, and the blood rushed through my ears.

Dying really sucks.

The light disappeared and I floated in darkness, surrounded by cold air that penetrated my skin and settled in my bones, numbing the excruciating pain from a few minutes before.

"You are mine." Arath's voice beckoned me and I struggled to open my eyes. I couldn't. It was like one of the blood dreams where I wanted to wake up but my brain would not cooperate.

"You are mine," he repeated. This time a hand pressed against my chest and my eyes behaved. It was difficult to focus at first, and I finally managed to stare into those burning yellow eyes. He was angry.

"What did I do now?" My voice came out in a hoarse whisper and it felt like glass was sliding up and down my throat.

"You almost died." He was gruff but squeezed me tight to his chest.

"Sorry." I smiled against his chest. He cared about me.

His hands pulled my hair back away from my face. "Don't do it again." He kissed me hard and it was as if he breathed new life into me. My skin tingled and warmed.

"Mmmm. Okay," I said against his lips. He pulled back and I saw that we were in his bedroom. The heavy curtains were drawn on his bed and Arath's incredible power swirled in silver and gold streaks around us.

"So why didn't you tell me you were, like, this powerfully cool mage?"

He laughed. "Cool?" His eyebrow went up. "I didn't want to frighten you."

291

"You can't scare me." At this he gave me one of his rare smiles. A new warmth, one that had nothing to do with his power, spread through me.

He hugged me again and then opened the curtain with a wave of his hand. My sisters stood around the bed chanting in a deep trance.

"I had some help," he admitted. "She is alive," his voice boomed again.

They opened their eyes. Tears streamed down their faces. Claire was dressed in her pajamas, Alex in a short, sequined minidress, and Mira in jeans and T-shirt that said "Mean for Green."

"Thanks for inviting me to the party." I grinned. My sisters piled on the bed and wrapped their arms around me, though Arath never let go.

"You scared the crap out of us, Gilly," Claire complained.

Alex nodded. "Almost dying is a really stupid thing to do."

I looked up at Arath. "So I've been told. How did I end up here?"

"Alex contacted me, and I brought them through the portal," Arath explained.

"I knew the minute the demon's poison grabbed your heart," said Mira.

I looked up at the king. "It was Clede, Arath. He betrayed you. And Emilio. What was he?"

"Darkness," Arath said.

"You killed him, just before you—" Mira stopped on a sob. She shook it off. "I'm with the rest of them. Don't do that again." She shook her finger at me. "I brought you back to the house and Arath opened the portal. He's kind of amazing." She stared up at the demon king.

"Yes, he is." He'd pulled me back from the brink of death, and I now understood how my mother felt.

"I brought you back where you belong. That is all that matters." He shifted and pulled me tighter to him.

The possessive nature of the move would have bothered me where most men were concerned, but not with Arath. I liked that he wanted me close. I smiled, and he returned the gesture with a slight grin.

"Is Bailey okay?" I turned to face my sisters.

"He's fine. Mom and Aunt Juliet are fussing over him. Mom's threatened to have him injected with a GPS chip so no matter where he is in the universe we can find him," Alex quipped.

I tried to laugh but it hurt, and I ended up coughing. "She shouldn't waste the time or the technology. He'd just find some way to disarm it."

"True that," Alex agreed.

Claire sighed. She was pale.

I looked at the other two. I frowned. "You guys need to go back and reenergize. This world is sucking away at your powers."

"We aren't leaving without you." Alex crossed her arms. Even though he'd saved my life, and our mother's, she still wasn't Arath's biggest fan.

"I'll be home soon, but I need to speak with Arath. I'm also not quite ready to hop back through the portal. I was just sucked back from God knows where through a vacuum-cleaner hose. At least that's what it felt like. Unlike you, I can draw power from here." *And Arath obviously has plenty to share.*

Mira leaned across and kissed my cheek. "Take your time." She pushed Claire off the enormous bed and grabbed Alex's hand. "Come on, twerps. We have some cleaning up to do." She meant that they had to purify their bodies.

"I promise, I'll be back soon." I waved at them.

My sisters walked to the door and touched their watches.

I was alone with Arath.

He still held me in his arms. I tried to shift up, but he wouldn't let me.

"So are you finished being angry with me?"

He shrugged nonchalantly. "I saved your life. I should think that would answer your question."

That made me laugh. "Why did you save me?"

He looked up at the ceiling as if asking for heavenly help.

"Please, tell me why you went to the trouble of saving me."

"You were betrayed by one of my people, and it was the least I could do." He frowned.

Please, let there be more. As much as I didn't want to admit it to myself I needed this man to want me as much as I did him. "Want" was too easy of a word. I loved him. As impossible as it might be, I wanted him to love me back. "Is that the only reason?"

"No." His face was clear of all emotion and I couldn't read him.

"Care to elaborate?"

"No."

I sighed. It was too much to hope for, and it was silly of me to ask. Expecting him to feel the same way as me was beyond ridiculous. The man ruled an entire world, and I had a feeling he could take over the universe if he wanted.

Enjoy it while you can. I remembered Claire's words. No one knew if we would win the fight against the darkness. It was time to make every moment count. Whatever Arath could give me I would take. I loved him enough for the both of us.

"I'm not sure how to say thank you. For saving me, and my mother, but I'll say it again any—" Before I could continue he kissed me. Not a gentle kiss, but an "I'm searching for your soul" kind of lip-lock. His arms squeezed me tight to his chest, so much so that I could barely breathe.

Then he let me go and I almost fell out of his lap. His

arm kept me from tumbling off the bed, my body feeling like I'd been warmed from the inside out. "I am fond of you, Guardian."

Fond was good. It wasn't love, but it was good. At least he wasn't mad at me anymore, and that was a start.

"I am fond of you, too. Very fond," I added.

He smiled and leaned back on the bed, stretching out. I felt brave and sexy. I moved so that I sat on his pelvis, and I could feel just how fond of me he was. That I had an effect on him gave me a sense of womanly power, the kind that had nothing to do with being a Guardian.

He reached up and brushed the hair from my face. "I knew the moment poison entered your body," he whispered. "My heart ached with your pain. If your sisters hadn't brought you to me, I would have gone after you myself."

Tears welled in my eyes and trickled onto my cheeks from the power of his words. He used his thumbs to wipe them away.

"Guardians don't cry." He smiled.

I shifted my weight to lean forward and I felt the length of him thicken. I kissed his lips. "I would have missed this," I whispered against his lips. I ran my hands across his chest and down his tight abs. "And this." I sighed.

He grabbed my hands and held them behind my back. "You are weak. I will not take advantage."

I leaned forward again, this time kissing his neck. "Funny, but I feel very much alive, and I don't see it as taking advantage. I see it as quenching a thirst." I used my teeth to tease his nipple.

He growled and rolled me over. "You must stop. I only have so much control where you are concerned." He was so serious it made me smile.

"Good," I whispered against his lips. "I want this. If you don't want me, tell me now, and I'll go home."

His hands moved to the sides of my face and his lips captured mine. "You are a frustrating woman, and I cannot tell you no."

In a matter of seconds we were both naked and his hands were doing delicious things to my body.

Sliding his hands from my breasts to my hips and lower, he drove me to the brink. When he touched my heat, I went over on a delicious ride.

He pulled me on top of him again and I guided him inside of me, well, as much of him as I could take. There was nothing small about the man.

There was something about the way he filled me so completely that once again sent me over the top. Then he began rocking his hips back and forth and I thought I might die from pleasure.

My hands leaned back on his thighs and I met him thrust for thrust, head thrown back, enjoying every sensation. His hands fondled my breasts, teasing my nipples to tight peaks. When it seemed as though I couldn't take one more second he exploded inside of me and we both cried out.

I fell against his chest almost weeping with release. I'd done a lot in my life, but I'd never experienced anything like this. I'd heard about people having a deeper connection, and I always thought it was a bunch of garbage. I was wrong.

It's because you love him.

I smiled against his chest.

"Now I'm really glad I didn't die, because I really would have missed that."

He chuckled. "You are a tease, Guardian, but you are my tease." Tugging at my hair, he kissed my neck and jaw, sending shivers of pleasure down my body. Then I felt him growing inside me again.

"You can't be serious!" I rose up to look into his eyes.

"My clan is known for stamina in all things. I'm a warrior."

"Oh my." I laughed as his hips began a slow rock against mine. "This is going to be interesting."

After the second time, I had no energy left.

"I could sleep for days," I said as I moved to his side. "I can't remember the last time I closed my eyes and didn't have some horrid dream." I still hadn't come to terms with the idea that it had been Emilio invading my dreams. Or at least the evil using him.

Arath waved a hand over my forehead and I instantly relaxed. "You're using magic on me again without my permission." I tried to be stern, but it didn't work. Whatever he did gave me a feeling of peace.

"Yes," he sighed. "It's time for you to rest. You need never fear to dream again, my Gillian. I will always protect my love," Arath whispered as I snuggled into his body.

CHAPTER

34

"Will my mother be there?" Arath zipped up the back of my dress. We were in my room at the house. The demon king was about to experience his first Thanksgiving with my family. I couldn't wait.

"Yes, she's back from her vacation. I think she finally put that Signor Batolli mess behind her. I hope so; I hate seeing her so sad." Turned out Batolli was the one who had killed Markie and the others. The big shocker was when we discovered he was Emilio's father, and also a Mantero. They both belonged to the secret society, which meant the evil hadn't chosen them at random. They'd both given themselves over to it.

It was Batolli who had been at the office when Markie and Reuben had met. He was the one who had pulled the computer expert over to the dark side. Unlike Batolli and Emilio, Reuben hadn't been willing. He was a pawn they controlled, and Markie and Jona had been caught in the crossfire.

The only thing we still hadn't figured out was what had happened to Emilio's paintings. We assumed Batolli took them to make it look like a robbery, but all of his homes had been searched and nothing turned up.

The murder in Paris made Aunt Juliet suspicious. She and Mom began researching and discovered the connection between the Batollis. The senior member had called Juliet from Paris the night of the murder, and that's how she figured it out. She and Mom tracked down the Italian investment banker and, well, he no longer exists. Juliet's Guardian skills came out of retirement.

Arath twisted one of my curls around his finger. "We were all betrayed in some way." Staring down at my feet, he smiled. "I like the sparkling shoes."

My choices in men hadn't become any less complicated, but I was definitely improving. Arath was a wonderful man, and I'd learned to enjoy every moment I had with him. Now that he'd been named head of the council, it was even easier to sneak in visits. Especially once he'd named me his personal bodyguard. I wasn't sure who was protecting whom, though. Sometimes I believed he wanted me around more so he could keep an eye on me, which was sweet in a way.

I laughed. "Me, too." I kissed him.

Here, in my room, it didn't feel like I was in love with a

powerful mage. He seemed very much like a handsome, caring man who smelled of cloves. It was even easy to forget he was a demon king. I had the feeling my dating days were over. *Thank God.* I didn't know if marriage was in our future, but there was already some kind of commitment.

I discovered, accidentally of course, that the demon king was supposed to have a harem of sorts to produce heirs. The subject had been brought up by Arath's new second in command, Bolenid, during a roundtable meeting I just happened to be attending on Maunra. The poor creature had nearly been beheaded for bringing it up in front of me.

It was only after I told Arath to spare the poor guy that he let him live. I will say, it made me feel good that the demon king didn't desire other women. After that meeting, he said I was worth thirty harems, and just as much trouble. He didn't have time for anyone else but me.

I took that as a compliment.

I slipped diamond studs into my ears, jewels he'd given me the previous week from his personal treasure.

He'd also helped me find and return as much of the stolen artifacts and jewels as we could find. We still hadn't found the link between the Amols and Arath's people, but we were working on it.

"Now, I know you're, like, Mr. Superdude and can handle anything, but I feel I have to warn you."

"Family dinners are a war zone." Arath repeated the words I'd said to him many times over the last few days since he'd received the invitation from my mother. "Expect the third degree, and don't get all red and flamey if someone picks on me. It only means they love me."

I couldn't keep from laughing when he said "flamey."

"You know"—I wrapped my arms around his neck—"I think you're going to fit right in."

Candace Havens is a veteran entertainment journalist who spends way too much time interviewing celebrities. In addition to her weekly column seen in newspapers throughout the country, she is the entertainment critic for 96.3 KSCS in the Dallas/Fort Worth area. She is the author of *Like a Charm, Charmed & Dangerous, Charmed & Ready, Charmed & Deadly,* and the nonfiction biography *Joss Whedon: Behind the Genius of Buffy,* as well as several published essays. Visit Candace at www.candacehavens.com.